A JUNIOR NOVELIZATION

by

Ellen Miles

Based on the motion picture screenplay
written by Deborah Kaplan & Harry Elfont
and Jim Cash & Jack Epps, Jr.

SCHOLASTIC INC.
New York   Toronto   London   Auckland   Sydney   Mexico City   New Delhi   Hong Kong

ISBN 0-439-17303-5

Designed by Peter Koblish

12 11 10 9 8 7 6 5 4 3 2 1   0 1 2 3 4 5 6/0
Printed in the U.S.A.
First Scholastic printing, May 2000

CHAPTER ONE
Introducing ... Me!

I am the great and powerful *Gazoo*, all know-ing, all seeing!

I am the great and powerful Gazoo, all know-ing, all seeing!

I *am* the great and powerful Gazoo, all know-ing, all seeing!

I am the *great* and *powerful* Gazoo, all — oh! Oh, dear, how embarrassing! I didn't see you there. I was just, um, practicing in this mirror here.

And the sorry truth is that while I am indeed great, I am not actually all that powerful. But I do know a lot. For example, I happen to know that you didn't wash behind your ears this morning. That's right, I'm talking to *you*! And I see a lot. I have ways of being everywhere at once. And ooh, the stories I could tell!

In fact, there's one I'd love to tell you right now. It's about a couple, a man and a woman. The kind of couple you think of as having been together for*ever*.

Who am I talking about? Take a deep breath. Are you sitting down? I'm talking about none other than Fred and Wilma. That's right, the Flintstones. Our favorite modern stone-age family. Can you believe there was ever a time when Fred and Wilma weren't living in their cozy stone hut together, barbecuing bronto burgers and playing peek-a-rock with Pebbles?

Well, believe it. Fred and Wilma are like any other couple, and their romance has a beautiful story of its own. It's not just gooey kissy stuff, either. This story has exotic locations, famous celebrities, jewel thieves, dancing girls, and all kinds of thrilling adventures along the way. And guess what? I, the great and power — I mean I, Gazoo, was there. In fact, I may just be partly responsible for getting our two lovebirds together! Want to hear all about it? Well, sit back and get ready to hear the greatest love story ever told: the story of Fred and Wilma.

It all started a few millennia ago when I was flying about in the mother ship — oh, did I neglect to tell you I'm an alien? I am. I'm on the short side, green of course, with a beautiful pair of silvery antennas sticking out of my head. Oh, and I have a rather large schnozzola. (That's alien for "nose.")

Anyway, there I was, minding my own business as my colleagues and I whizzed through space on one of our regular fact-finding trips (we are a peaceful race, but curious about the ways of other beings). I was staring out the window, watching the stars race by, when suddenly I heard my commander calling me.

"Kazoo!" he bellowed.

See what I have to put up with?

"Actually," I informed him with utmost courtesy, "it's *Guh*-zoo. *Guh.* Shall we say it together?"

He ignored me. "Silence!" he bellowed again. He gestured to an underling, who stepped forward. "Inform Kazoo about his latest posting," he ordered.

The underling read from a screen that

popped down in front of his eyes. "Because of your poor past performance as an intergalactic observer —"

I interrupted. "Wait! What are you talking about?" I asked. They're always picking on me.

The commander bellowed again. "I asked for silence!" he repeated. "We're talking about the fact that you have no professional detachment. You get involved. You can't keep that huge schnozz of yours out of everybody's business. And furthermore —"

His yelling was beginning to hurt my ears. "Okay, okay," I said. "I think I get the point."

The commander gestured to the underling, who continued to read. ". . . we are sending you to a planet where there is virtually no civilization for you to mess up."

"No!" I cried. "Not —" It couldn't be. They wouldn't, would they?

"Earth." Both the commander and his underling spoke at once.

I nearly fainted.

"You will document the earthlings' bizarre rituals of love and marriage," the underling went on, with absolutely no regard for my feelings.

The commander shook his head. "I just can't understand why they can't reproduce the way we do," he said. As he spoke, he split in half, creating a small but perfectly identical version of himself. The underling looked at the tiny new commander admiringly.

"It's a boy!" he said.

"And so green and slimy," I added.

"Oh, stop kissing up," said the commander. He gestured once more, and another underling appeared, trundling one of our PS3's (Personal Saucers, third version). "Hop in." The commander held the lid open for me.

What choice did I have? I hopped in. "But wait!" I said, as they closed the lid down. "Aren't there others far more qualified than I —?"

"Of course," answered the commander, locking down the lid. "But why risk losing one of them?"

He and the underling got a big laugh out of that one. They shoved me toward the hatch.

"Wait!" I yelled, my voice echoing inside the PS3. "You can't send me to earth. They're prehistoric down there. They haven't even invented pants yet! You can't send me to a pantless planet. Haven't you ever seen my legs?"

5

They just kept laughing.

"Imagine the poor moron who gets stuck with Gazoo," said the underling, as he and the commander gave me one last push through the hatch.

And that was the last thing I heard as I hurtled out into space, whizzing at Mach 25 toward that blue-and-white marble known as earth.

CHAPTER TWO
Hello Fred, Hello Wilma

As I hurtled, I used my scanner to comb earth's population. Object? To find likely subjects for observation. I'd show that commander. This time I'd do a *fabulous* job. And I wouldn't get personally involved. Not me. Not Gazoo. No matter what.

"Yes!" I cried, as I spotted a pair of earthlings driving along in an incredibly primitive foot-powered vehicle. "Perfect." One was large, with dark fur on his head and a huge, square jaw. The other was small and had lighter head-fur.

These beings were to become known to me as Fred Flintstone and Barney Rubble, average earthlings inhabiting the town of Bedrock. I

7

zoomed in on them to listen in on their conversation. . . .

"Hey, Barney," said Fred as their car paused at a Hoperoo Crossing and then drove over a bronto-bridge, "this sure is an exciting time for us, isn't it?"

Fred smiled over at Barney as they drove through the looming stone gates of their school: Brontocrane Academy.

"Uh, sure, Fred," said Barney, uncertainly.

"I figured out exactly how to ace our final exam," Fred said as they entered the school locker room. He picked up his tortoiseshell hard hat and stuck it on his head. "See all these other mugs?" He gestured around at their classmates. "They're gonna stay up all night studying, right?"

"Uh, Fred . . ." Barney looked as if he had something to say.

"Don't interrupt, Barn! Then, when they finally do get to sleep, the information's just gonna fall right outta their heads! Now me," Fred said, puffing up his chest, "I'm way ahead of everybody. See, I'm not gonna study tonight. I'm gonna get a good night's rest, get up extra-early, and study in the *morning*! That way, everything will still be right up front in my noggin by the time I get to work to take the test tomorrow." He tapped his forehead.

"That's a great plan, Fred," Barney seemed to agree. "Except for one thing. The test is today."

Fred stared at Barney. "Today?"

By then they had arrived in the main practice area. Other trainees were already mounted on their brontocranes, nervously working the levers as a team of examiners with clipboards watched closely. Barney pointed at a sign that said "Bronto Crane Testing Today." There was no question about it. Barney was right.

"FLINTSTONE!" someone bellowed.

Fred whirled around to see one of the examiners pointing right at him.

"You're next!" said the examiner.

Fred gulped.

"Don't worry, Fred," Barney said, patting him on the back. "You'll do fine. "I've got my mechanic's test today, too. It'll be a breeze."

"Sure, sure," Fred muttered. He climbed up onto his bronto and looked over the levers. It was as if he'd never seen them before, even though he'd just finished a full course in learning all about them.

"Back her up," instructed the examiner.

Fred grabbed a lever. The bronto lurched forward, breaking off a huge chunk of rock and sending it hurtling to the quarry floor. "Did you say back up?" Fred asked, with a nervous laugh. "I thought you said *break* up. Oops."

The examiner didn't say a thing. He just shook his head and chiseled some notes onto his stone clipboard.

Fred realized it was now or never. Shape up or ship out. Pass — or fail. "Get a grip," he told himself. But it wasn't until Barney reappeared, having quickly finished his test, that Fred began to feel himself again. It meant a lot to Fred to have his best friend there for support.

"Way to go, Fred!" Barney cried, as Fred maneuvered huge boulders into baskets of different sizes.

"That's it!" declared the examiner, checking his sundial for the time.

"How'd I do?" asked Fred anxiously.

The examiner added up the marks on his clipboard. "You passed," he said finally.

"Yabba dabba —" Fred let go of the controls as he cheered. In that split second a boulder fell from the bronto's mouth and landed right on top of the examiner, drilling him into the ground. "Oooh," Fred finished, much more quietly.

Later, Fred and Barney received their diplomas. Afterwards, while all the other graduates hugged their families and posed for pictures, Fred wandered about, looking a little sad. Somehow, graduating from Bronto Crane Academy just wasn't as fulfilling as it could have been. Something was missing. Or, should I say, some*one*?

Meanwhile, far away in the biggest mansion on the highest hillside overlooking the town of Bedrock, a bridal shower was taking place. The mansion was the home of Pearl Slaghoople, her husband the Colonel, and their daughter, Wilma.

The bride to be? Wilma's cousin Rockquel. She sat with her guests, giggling and drinking tea as she worked her way through an enormous stack of presents. "Oooh!" she cried, ripping the paper off a huge box, which she opened to reveal a small, scaly dinosaur with a long, hoselike trunk. "A vacuum cleaner! *Kisses*, Kitty! It's exactly what I wanted. Except for the color . . ."

After reaching over to bestow several air kisses on her friend, Rockquel set down the vacuum next to a juicer (a baby dino with a hard head for squeezing fruit) and a garbage disposal (a slop-eating dino-pig). Immediately the three creatures started talking among themselves, muttering about how long Rockquel's marriage would last.

"Wilma, isn't that just the cutest vacuum cleaner?" Rockquel asked. "Wilma?" She looked around. "Where's Wilma?"

Pearl Slaghoople, sitting nearby, heaved a huge sigh. "I can guess," she said. She stood up and adjusted her designer gown. "I'll go look for her."

Sure enough, Pearl found Wilma out on the balcony upstairs. "Wilma, your sister is looking for you. She wants you at her shower," Pearl said.

"Oh, Mother. You know I can't stand that sort of thing. So boring. Who cares about all that junk?" She turned her gaze back to the view: the town of Bedrock, spread out far below the mansion. Wilma was a pretty girl, with long blond curly hair. She was wearing a simple white dress. She looked lovely — but sad.

"Wilma Slaghoople!" Pearl exclaimed. "Are

you staring at that tar pit, Bedrock, again? There's nothing down there but a bunch of flat-footed, flat-headed Neanderthals grunting and clubbing each other. I mean, they're still afraid of *fire* down there!" She bent over and swung her arms to shield her face, imitating a Bedrockian. "Ahh, ahhh! Make it go away!" she grunted.

"Mother!" cried Wilma. "They're people, no different from you or me." She couldn't stand how her mother made fun of anyone who wasn't as wealthy as the Slaghooples.

Pearl rolled her eyes. "This is all my fault," she said. "I never should have let you play with the servants' children. Now come on, let's go back downstairs to that shower. You can at least pretend to have fun, like everybody else."

Wilma gave one more wistful glance back at Bedrock. "Yes, Mother," she said.

Downstairs, the party was in full swing.

"Look!" cried Rockquel, just as Wilma and Pearl came into the room. "Oven mitts!"

"Big whoop," Wilma muttered, under her breath. But she flashed a smile at Rockquel. She could at least try to be supportive of her cousin, and pretend to join in her happiness.

"Well, that's it for presents," said Rockquel. "What shall we do next?"

"How about going for a drive?" asked Wilma.

"Sure!" cried Kitty. "To the club, for tea!"

"I was thinking of going someplace new," Wilma confessed. "We could do something different, something fun. Like — we could go to Bedrock and go bowling!"

There was a dead silence in the room. Then, all at once, everybody burst out laughing.

"Oh, Wilma," Rockquel said finally, wiping away tears. "You *are* a hoot!"

Wilma frowned, but nobody noticed.

"She's the best," Rockquel told her friends. "Isn't she just the best?"

"She sure is." At the sound of a male voice, every head in the room whipped around. The girls sighed when they saw Chip Rockefeller, Wilma's boyfriend. Chip was tall, handsome, and very, very rich. "That's my Wilma," he said, bending to kiss Wilma's hand. "Beautiful *and* witty. A prize for any man."

The girls sighed again. All except for Wilma.

"Chip, what are you doing here?" she asked.

He gave her a little grin. "I stopped by to discuss some business with Colonel Slaghoople." He winked at Wilma. "There's a certain girl I'm thinking of investing in."

He took off as Rockquel's friends giggled.

"Well," said Rockquel, raising her eyebrows, "I guess the next bridal shower will be Wilma's."

"Don't start chiseling the invitations yet." Wilma slumped into her seat. The idea of marrying Chip was anything but thrilling. Wilma was tired of her boring, privileged life. She wanted something different, something exciting.

"What are you saying?" asked Rockquel. "You can't let a man like Chip slip through your fingers. Why, he was first in his class at Princestone!"

"And he owns half of Rock Vegas!" added Kitty. "The biggest entertainment center in the known world!"

Wilma sighed. She glanced into the other room and saw Chip and her father talking together. Chip put his arm around the Colonel's shoulder, as if they were good buddies. Wilma sighed again.

"Come on, Wilma," said Rockquel. "You and Chip are perfect for each other. Just think of the fabulous life you'll lead when you're married to somebody that rich: playing tennis, shopping —"

"Getting facials!" chimed in Kitty. "You'll be just like your mother."

That did it. Wilma jumped to her feet and started running. And she didn't stop until she was far, far away from the Slaghoople mansion.

CHAPTER THREE
Haven't We Met?

I know, I know. You're wondering when I, Gazoo, will come into the story. Well, be patient. It won't be long now.

Back in Bedrock, Fred was walking around by himself in the dark, tossing stones into the quarry. The graduation celebration was over, but Fred didn't feel like going home to the trailer he shared with Barney.

"Fred!" said Barney, coming up behind him. "I've been looking all over for you."

"I didn't feel much like celebrating," Fred told him, looking glum.

"Are you kidding?" asked Barney. "We get to work in this quarry for the rest of our lives! Who says dreams don't come true?" He whirled around, gesturing at the mounds of rock and sand surrounding them.

Fred just sighed. "I know I should be happy. I just wish I had somebody special to share my success with."

"You got me, Fred." Barney smiled up at him.

"Thanks, Barn. But that's not really what I'm talking about."

"Yeah, I know." Barney paused. "Um, what *are* you talking about?"

"A girl, Barney. A girl."

"Right, right," said Barney. "Hey, don't worry, Fred. You'll meet somebody when you least expect it." Barney hated to see his friend so down in the dumps.

"I don't know, Barn. I think you have to make things happen. I mean, it's not like something's gonna drop outta the sky right in front of you and change your whole life." Fred heaved another sigh.

Do I hear my cue? This is where I, Gazoo, enter. Stage right. Or, actually, stage up. At that very moment, my PS3 streaked across the sky, lighting up everything within miles, and dropped into the sand with a loud crash, right in front of Barney and Fred. Ahh, a perfect landing. Well, *almost* perfect. I tried the lid, but it wouldn't open. "Help!" I called. My voice echoed inside the saucer.

"Fred!" Barney cried, alarmed. "I think somebody's in there!"

"C'mon," said Fred. "Let's try to open it up." He grabbed the first thing he saw: my antennas, which stick up out of the PS3 when it's closed. He tugged and tugged — then fell over backward as I popped free.

Fred looked into the bottom of my saucer. "I dunno, Barn," he said. "It looks empty." He was still hanging onto my antennas.

"Would you mind not grabbing me by the antennas?" I piped up. "It's not an altogether pleasant sensation."

Fred looked down. What he'd thought was the top of the ship was actually my *helmet*. "Yow!" he cried, tossing me as far as he could!

I tumbled along until I could catch myself. Then I floated back to them, brushing myself off. It was already painfully clear that I hadn't picked the *brightest* Bedrockians to observe.

"Wh — what are you?" Fred asked.

"I am the Great Gazoo," I answered politely.

"The great Kazoo?" Barney asked.

I sighed. "*Guh*-zoo," I corrected him. "I come from a planet too far away for you to fathom and a civilization too advanced for you to comprehend . . ."

"Hey!" Barney interrupted. "I bet we get wishes!"

"Pardon?" I asked.

"We let you outta your fancy bottle. Now we get wishes."

"Yeah!" shouted Fred. "And the first thing I'm gonna wish for is more wishes."

"Smart." Barney nodded admiringly. "I was just gonna wish for more toes."

"Okay," said Fred, turning back to me. "Where do we rub?"

I stared at him. "Is there any *intelligent* life around here for me to speak to?"

"What's that supposed to mean?"

"Look," I said patiently. "I'm not some cartoon genie. And that's not a bottle. It's a spacecraft. I'm from a highly evolved alien species!"

They looked disappointed. But it was time to set the record straight.

"I don't do funny voices, I don't sing catchy songs, and I don't have a magic carpet. I'm just here to observe your mating rituals. Got it, Dum-dums?"

"Dum-dums? Is that some kind of insult?" Fred asked.

"If the shoe fits . . ." I said.

"What's a shoe?" asked Barney.

Oh, dear. I rolled my eyes. "Yes, it was an insult."

That was when Fred started swinging his fists at me. How primitive — not to mention inefficient. I simply floated around his punches. Was it my fault that Barney managed to walk right into one instead? That's when I decided to take off. Later, Fred and Barney!

CHAPTER FOUR
Fred Gets a Date

While I was meeting up with Fred and Barney, Wilma was wandering through the streets of downtown Bedrock. She was charmed by all the activity. There were street vendors, deliverymen, bicyclists pedaling along, sailors getting tattoos at outdoor stands . . .

It was all pretty thrilling for a rich girl who'd lived a very sheltered life in the hills far above Bedrock.

But Wilma was getting tired — and hungry. She'd run away from Rockquel's shower hours and hours ago, and she was ready for a rest. Her nose led her to the nearest restaurant, a noisy, colorful outdoor joint with a huge neon sign that shouted

BRONTO KING. Waitresses on skates whizzed around as music blared through the loudspeakers.

"Wow," said Wilma, taking it all in. Everybody looked so happy! There were no stuffy waiters, no starched white tablecloths, no fancy silverware. Just good food and lots of it, and plenty of fun people to eat with.

"Hi, darlin'," bubbled a cute, dark-haired girl who had just skated up to Wilma. "Have a seat and take a look at a menu, why don't you? I'm Betty, and I'll be your waitress." She grinned at Wilma. "What'll it be?"

"Oh!" said Wilma, flustered. "I was just — I mean, I, um . . ." She looked down at the menu. "Well, how much is a glass of water?"

"Water? That's free," answered Betty.

"Oh," said Wilma. "Then I'll have two, please." Wilma had left home in such a hurry that she didn't have a cent on her. Just then, another waitress skated by carrying a huge tray of steaming Bronto Burgers. Wilma eyed it hungrily.

Betty followed Wilma's eyes. "You want a burger to go with your water?" she asked.

"What?" replied Wilma, surprised. "Oh, no. I'm just — water's fine."

"Because if you're short on cash or something," Betty went on, "I could help out. You could pay me back later, when you have a chance to go home and get your wallet."

Wilma looked sad. "No, no — I mean, thanks, but no. I can't. I mean, I can't — go home." The mansion in the hills suddenly didn't feel like home anymore. Wilma wanted more out of life than the things money could buy.

"Oh, no!" Betty said sympathetically. "Are you — caveless? You poor thing. I mean — I'm sorry, I just called you poor. That's awful. I mean, you're just down on your luck, right?" Betty looked terribly upset.

"I —"

Betty didn't notice that Wilma was trying to correct her.

"Don't you worry about a thing," she went on. "You can stay with me until you're back on your feet. And I'm going to buy you lunch. And I bet I can get you a job here, too."

"Oh!" Wilma cried. "That's so nice. But I'm not a charity case —"

"I understand. I used to volunteer at the caveless shelter. I saw all kinds of people there. Anyway, I won't take no for an answer. By the way, I'm Betty. Betty O'Shale." She held out her hand.

"I'm Wilma. Wilma Slag — I mean, Slaghoo — feldsparstein. You can just call me Wilma." Betty was being so nice. Wilma didn't have the heart to tell her the truth just then.

"Let's get you some food. Then we can go on up to my apartment," Betty said.

"You live in an *apartment*?" asked Wilma, excited. "How cool! I always wondered what it would be like to live in an apartment."

Betty shook her head sadly, then gave Wilma a huge hug. "Life can be so cruel sometimes," she said to herself as she skated off to get Wilma a burger.

I visited Fred and Barney again that night, floating into the little box they live in, just as they were saying goodnight to each other. This time, Fred didn't try to punch me. Maybe he was just too tired. Instead, he told me how hard it was to find "goils" to meet. As I understood it, meeting "goils" is a first step in the human marriage procedure.

We ended up at Bronto King the very next night.

The place was hopping. Every table was full, and the waitresses were working hard to keep up. Betty skated around with ease, carrying her heavy tray high. Wilma, on the other hand, was having a little trouble. Just as we pulled up, I saw a major Wilma wipe-out. Fortunately, she wasn't hurt. And fortunately for her customers, Betty grabbed her tray just in time and saved the Bronto Burgers.

Fred and Barney gaped at all the waitresses.

"So, here are the goils," I pointed out. "Get busy you two."

"Shh!" Fred gave me an angry look. "You're gonna cramp our style."

"Style?" I snickered. "Listen, dum-dum . . ." (I know it's not nice to call names. But with these two, I just can't help myself sometimes!)

"Enough with the dum-dum!" shouted Fred. "My name's Fred Flintstone! F-L-I-N —" He paused for a second.

"T," offered Barney.

"STONE!" finished Fred, shaking a finger at me.

"I don't care who you are," said an old man standing nearby. "Quit shouting at me."

"I'm not shouting at you," Fred shouted. "I'm talking to this guy."

"Who, him?" the man asked, pointing at Barney.

"No, him." Fred pointed at me. "The little green guy."

The old man gave Fred a funny look.

Then Fred gave Barney a funny look. "Oh, no," he said. "We're the only ones who can see him! We've been talking to Gazoo all day, and everybody probably thought we were a couple of —"

"Dum-dums?" I asked, floating out of reach before he could make me into a punching bag.

Fred and Barney watched as Betty skated up to a car — boy did she get a surprise then. Right there in the front seat she saw her boyfriend Stoney kissing another girl! Betty dumped a milkshake over his head and skated off. Fred and Barney couldn't help admiring her for that.

"You know, Barney," said Fred. "I got a good feeling that today could be my day. Why, I could turn around right now and meet the girl of my dreams."

27

Just then, Wilma skated past, way out of control. Fred didn't even notice her. But he *definitely* noticed Betty when she skated up to take their order. Right then, he made up his mind to ask her on a date.

"What'll it be, boys?"

Fred gave Barney a glance. "Watch this," he said, with a superior look. Then he turned back to Betty. "Um . . ." He was speechless. His mouth hung open. Suddenly, he couldn't get a single word out. "Mr. Smooth" had just turned into Mr. Loser.

Betty raised an eyebrow.

Still speechless, Fred pointed to himself, then to Betty.

Betty had seen Fred's type before. She knew he could use a little extra help. Besides, after just seeing her boyfriend with another girl, Betty was ready to move on — fast. "Oh, you want a date?" she asked.

Fred nodded.

"Okay, you can take me to the carnival tomorrow."

Fred looked stunned. "Uh . . . um . . ." Just then, Barney pulled on Fred's tunic.

Betty noticed. "Your friend seems to want a

date, too. No problem. I got the perfect girl." At that exact moment, there was a huge crash behind them. "Don't worry, I'm sure she'll be fine by then!" Betty sang out, as she skated off to rescue Wilma and tell her about their big double date.

And that, my friends, is how it all began.

CHAPTER FIVE
The Dating Begins

I could hardly wait to observe a human "date." But in truth, the whole thing was pretty disappointing at first. I rode along in the car as Fred and Barney picked up the "goils." Betty got into the front seat with Fred, and Wilma joined Barney in back. And then? Nobody said a *word* for a long, long time. Betty and Fred pretended to smile at each other, while in the back seat Barney, *way* shorter than Wilma, was too shy to even glance at her.

"I may not know much about your courting rituals," I whispered in Fred's ear, "but I'll go out on a limb and say this can't be going very well."

Fred made a face at me.

Things hadn't improved much by the time

they got to the carnival. Wilma's eyes grew round as she looked around at all the rides and games. She watched in awe as screaming carloads of people rode the roller coaster: three brontos, linked together. "Wow," she said. "It all looks like so much fun! And look at the games. There's a bowling one. Barney, could we go bowling?"

"I guess," said Barney reluctantly. "Fred and I go all the time."

Fred pointed to a sign. COMING SOON: JURASSIC PARK — THE RIDE!

"That's just silly," he said. "Who's gonna pay to see dinosaurs, when we've all got 'em in our backyards?"

Barney cracked up.

So did Betty.

They both had the goofiest laughs.

They stared at each other. Suddenly, it was as if their friends didn't exist. "Hey, do you like roller coasters?" Betty asked.

"I'll race you to it," Barney responded immediately.

And they were off like a shot.

That left Fred and Wilma standing there looking at each other.

"This is going to be fun, huh?" asked Wilma. Fred shrugged.

"What do you want to do first?"

Fred shrugged again. "Uh, what was your name again?" he asked.

I smacked my forehead. This was *not* going well at all.

Wilma asked Fred if they could try some games, since she wasn't quite ready for the roller coaster.

First they tried the dunk 'em booth, then the test-your-strength booth, then the shooting gallery. Finally, Wilma got her wish: They stopped at the bowling booth.

Fred, using his weird-in-a-cute-way "twinkle toes" approach, wowed Wilma with his expertise. He even won a huge dinosaur egg to take home. Then Wilma asked him to teach her how to bowl. As he showed her how to roll the ball, they touched — and suddenly I could have sworn I saw sparks. With Fred's help, Wilma knocked down all the pins. The two of them were hugging when Barney ran up.

"Hey, Fred," he said. "I'm sorry I sorta ran off with Betty. I know Wilma was my date, but . . ."

"No problem," said Fred, before Barney could finish. "See you later — and have fun!" As soon as Barney left, Fred turned to Wilma. "How about a ride on the Ferris wheel?" he asked. Finally! Mr. Romance was on the right track. Even I, an alien, could tell that the Ferris wheel was a great place to take a goil.

Soon they were high above the carnival, gazing down at the lights and listening to the sounds of music that drifted toward them from below.

"Gee, it's kind of chilly all of a sudden," said Wilma. "I sure wish there was *something* I could drape around my shoulders."

Fred looked blank for a minute. "Oh!" he said, finally taking the hint. He put his arm around her.

That's when I showed up. "Nice work, lover-boy," I congratulated him. "I guess my work here is almost done."

"I'm ignoring you," Fred said, gritting his teeth.

"What?" asked Wilma.

"I — uh — I said I'm *adoring* you."

Wilma shut her eyes and sighed, leaning her head on Fred's big shoulder. "Oh, Fred," she

33

said. "For a tough guy, you're just the sweetest thing."

Fred just sat there like a lump.

"Come on!" I cried. I blinked, and a little space harp appeared in my hands. I strummed it and sang along. "La, la, la, isn't it romantic. Now hurry up and kiss her, dum —"

Fred shoved me right off the ride, smiled at Wilma, and leaned closer. "Your eyes are like . . . two big . . . eyes," he said. He was puckering up his lips, getting ready to kiss her (finally!) when the egg he'd won at the bowling booth started to crack. Something was hatching!

Just as Fred's and Wilma's lips were about to meet, the egg popped open. An adorable purple dinosaur pup jumped out of it and started licking Fred — right on the mouth! Fred's eyes opened wide.

"Eccchhh!" he cried.

"Oh, he's so cute," Wilma cooed. "And he must think you're his mother."

The dinosaur squirmed with joy. Wilma just giggled as Fred tried to get him to stay down.

That chance for a kiss was over. On the way home, Wilma told him he wasn't like the guys she'd grown up with. She said she liked how Fred wasn't out to impress her, and how he just wanted to have fun.

At Betty's door, Wilma told Fred what a great time she'd had. The baby dinosaur, which they'd already named Dino, was romping around on the vine leash they'd made for him. "Well, good night," Fred said awkwardly. Should he kiss her? He wasn't sure.

"Good night," said Wilma.

"Good night," said Fred again.

(I was dying! Wasn't he *ever* going to get around to kissing her?)

Finally, he stuck out his hand for a shake. (Oh, please!) At the same moment, Dino began running around like crazy, and his leash wound around the two of them, pulling them oh-so-close together.

It was almost as if they had no choice.

Fred and Wilma kissed.

Afterwards, Wilma went inside and closed the door. She leaned against it with a contented sigh — just as everything in Betty's apartment began to shake from the sound of Fred's eardrum-shattering happy shout, "Yabba-Dabba Doo!"

That was just the first date. After that, the ice was broken and Fred and Wilma and Barney and Betty did everything together. They watched videos, they went on picnics, they had their pictures taken . . . Fred and Wilma even talked a little about what it would be like to have a house of their own someday. Fred and Barney were convinced they'd found the girls of their dreams. (Naturally, I was happy. I was taking plenty of notes for the commander. I knew he'd be pleased with my report. Maybe I'd even get a promotion this time!)

Wilma and Betty were happy, too. One night, while they were putting on mud masks — some "goil" ritual, I deduced — they chattered about how good life was. Wilma told Betty how much she owed her for taking her in and introducing her to Fred. Betty told Wilma she deserved a few breaks, after the rough life she'd had.

Wilma took a deep breath. Maybe it was finally time to tell Betty the truth about herself. "Actually, Betty," she began, "there's something about me you should know —"

Just then, the doorbell rang.

"Is that the pizza delivery boy already?" asked Betty.

She opened the door.

Pearl Slaghoople was standing there, dressed to the teeth and dripping with jewels, as usual.

"Mother!" cried Wilma.

"Wilma!" cried Pearl, staring at Wilma's muddy face. "My poor baby! What's happened to my little girl?" She looked around the messy apartment. "Good heavens!"

"What are you doing here?" asked Wilma.

Pearl didn't answer. She stared at Betty, whose face was still covered with mud. "Who are you? The cleaning lady? Obviously, you're doing a terrible job. You're fired!"

"Mother!" cried Wilma. "This is my new best friend, Betty."

Pearl raised an eyebrow.

"Wilma," said Betty tactfully, "I'm going to go take a bath. Nice to meet you, Mrs. Slaghoofeldsparstein."

"What did she call me?" Pearl asked as Betty scurried into the bathroom.

Wilma ignored the question. She still couldn't believe her mother was there. "Mother, how did you find me?"

"I hired a detective," confessed Pearl. "Now let's go home."

"I *am* home," Wilma declared. "And if you force me to go back to that mansion, I'll just run away again." She folded her arms and gave Pearl a stubborn glare.

"Fine, Wilma," said Pearl. "Go ahead and break *my* heart. But I won't let you break your father's. He misses you terribly, and if you aren't there for his birthday party on Sunday . . ."

Wilma felt a pang of guilt. "Okay," she said, after some thought. "I'll come. But I'm going to bring some of my new friends with me."

"Like who, the cleaning lady?" asked Pearl.

"Her name's Betty."

"Whatever," said Pearl. "I don't think so, dear. We've only invited the cream of society."

"Then I'm not coming." Wilma folded her arms.

"Oh, all right," said Pearl. "Bring your friends. Just remember, it's black tie." She leaned over to kiss Wilma, but couldn't find a mud-free spot. She settled for an air kiss. Then she left.

Wilma gulped. So far, she'd enjoyed every minute of her romance with Fred. But now it was time for a little reality check. What were her new friends going to think when they found out who she really was?

CHAPTER SIX
Wilma's Secret Life

I caught up with Fred and Barney as they left for the party on Sunday night. Boy, did they look dopey in their monkey suits!

"Jeez," Fred was saying, "I wonder why Wilma gave us these clothes to wear for the party."

"Maybe it's a costume party," Barney guessed.

"Oooh, what fun!" I said, popping into view.

"Hey, Gazoo, do you really have to come with us?" Fred asked. "Nothing personal, but you know what they say: two and a half's a crowd."

"Please," I said. "The truth is, I find observing you dum-dums going all ga-ga to be simply ho-hum." I yawned. "I would prefer to observe you earning your daily bread or hurling spears at woolly mammoths. But as it is, I have no choice but to suffer your romantic misadventures with you."

"Well, just try to stay out of our hair!" Fred glared at me.

"No problem," I said. His hair looked as if it hadn't been shampooed in months. I would be happy to stay out of it.

Just before they left, Fred chained Dino to a tree. "Stay, Dino!" he commanded. "Stay!"

Dino whimpered a little as Fred and Barney got into their car and drove off. He yanked at his chain, but it wouldn't budge.

On the way to the party, Fred pulled something out of his pocket to show Barney. "What do you think, Barn?" he asked. He popped open the clamshell box to reveal a sparkling engagement ring.

"Oh, Fred, you shouldn't have." Barney reached for the ring.

Fred grabbed it back. "It's not for you, nitwit! It's for Wilma. I'm gonna ask her to marry me!"

I popped in to take a closer look at the ring. A special magnifying glass flipped down from my helmet, and I squinted hard. "Oh, dear!" I quipped.

"It appears that a tiny flake of something is stuck right there on your ring . . ." I couldn't help making fun of the minuscule diamond.

Fred closed the box. "Thanks a lot," he grumbled. "That's the stone. It's all I could afford."

"Oh." I cleared my throat. "Well, I'm sure she'll be very impressed by your . . . frugality."

"But see, that's the thing about Wilma," Fred told me and Barney. "I don't feel the need to impress her at all. She's just a simple girl with simple tastes."

Barney and I nodded. And I, Gazoo, kept my mouth shut. (Wasn't that polite of me?)

The boys stopped at Betty's to pick up Betty and Wilma. The girls — Wilma elegant in white and Betty adorable in blue — looked terrific and Fred's and Barney's eyes nearly fell out at the sight of them. Those goils were something else! Then they drove on, with Wilma giving directions, up the winding road into the hills. Finally, they drove through the huge gates that marked the driveway to Slaghoople Manor.

Fred, Barney, and Betty looked up at the mansion, so unlike any of the modest homes in Bedrock. Then they turned to stare at Wilma.

"You know," she said, with a nervous giggle,

"I guess there are a few things I haven't quite gotten around to telling you guys . . ."

Betty looked mad. As soon as Fred pulled up in front of the mansion, she got out of the car and slammed the door shut behind her.

"Betty, wait!" cried Wilma. She got out of the car, too, and ran after Betty. "I tried to tell you. I was just so ashamed."

"I can see why," said Betty sarcastically, nodding toward the huge, beautiful mansion.

"Please, Betty, I hope you don't think too badly of me."

"Of course I don't," said Betty, even though she was obviously furious. "I just feel so dumb. I should have realized a caveless girl couldn't afford the designer clothes you wear."

"Oh, Betty..." Wilma began, but just then a woman draped in furs and jewels rushed up to hug her.

"Wilma, dahling!" cried the woman. "You look divine! Look, everybody, it's Wilma!"

A crowd of guests clustered around Wilma. Betty just stood there, watching.

Meanwhile, in the car, Fred was crestfallen. "Barney," he moaned. "She's loaded!"

"Looks that way, Fred. I guess you really lucked out, huh?"

"No, Barn! Don't you see? This is *terrible!*" Fred was staring down at the little clamshell box he'd pulled out of his pocket. "I can't give her this measly little ring! Look at that house! A girl who grew up there is used to the best of everything. She'd take one look at this ring and laugh her head off. You know, Barney, it's a good thing I didn't have the chance to give it to her sooner." He tossed the box into the glove compartment. Then he got out of the car.

Just then, a man in a fancy uniform jumped into Fred's car and started to drive off.

"Hey! What are you doing?" Fred yelled. "Help! This guy's trying to steal my car."

The crowd of people near Wilma all turned to stare. The uniformed man shushed Fred. "No, sir, you don't understand. I'm the valet."

Fred gave him a threatening look. "The ballet? I don't care if you're going to the opera, pal. You're not going in *my* car!"

Barney tried to hold Fred back. Wilma and Betty ran over, too. "Fred," said Wilma. "He's the valet. It's his job to park your car."

"I knew that," Fred answered quickly, with a little laugh.

The other guests rolled their eyes.

Wilma took Fred's arm and led him toward the house.

Meanwhile, back at Fred and Barney's trailer, Dino was still pulling at his chain. He couldn't stand being left behind! All he wanted was to be with Fred. He struggled and grunted and struggled some more. His face turned an even darker purple from the effort, and drops of sweat flew off his forehead. Finally, the tree began to bend. Dino grinned and pulled harder. Suddenly, the whole tree came up by its roots!

Dino jumped for joy. Then he took off down the road to find Fred, bounding happily along — with the whole tree, roots and all, dragging along behind him.

CHAPTER SEVEN
A Chip Off the Old Block

The backyard of the Slaghoople mansion was beautifully decorated for the Colonel's birthday, with balloons and streamers everywhere. Waiters circulated with trays of food and drinks while a piano-playing orangutan provided background music.

Pearl spotted Fred and Wilma as soon as they entered the yard. "Wilma!" she yoo-hooed. "There you are!" Turning to the Colonel, she added in a lower voice, "Oh, dear, she really did bring her friends."

Wilma and Fred crossed the beautiful lawn toward Pearl and the Colonel. "Happy Birthday, Daddy," said Wilma, kissing him.

The Colonel smiled at her. He was dressed in

his best uniform, complete with a sword at his side and a monocle screwed into one eye. "Yes, yes," he said vaguely. "News from the front?" The Colonel seemed a little out of it. He behaved as if he were still in the army, ordering troops about and making strategy for the next battle.

"Morale is excellent," Wilma reported, humoring him. Then she turned to Fred. "Mother, Daddy, I'd like you to meet my new boyfriend, Fred."

Fred stuck out a hand to shake with the Colonel. But the Colonel just saluted and marched out of the room.

Fred looked confused, but he stuck out his hand to Pearl instead. She took it for just a second, them pulled away. "Lovely," she murmured, insincerely. "Wilma, there's someone here who's dying to see you. Chip! Oh, Chip!"

Fred turned to see a handsome man in an expensive-looking black suit striding toward them. The crowd parted to let him through.

"Mother!" cried Wilma, dismayed. "You invited Chip?"

"Of course," Pearl answered. "He's practically family."

"Who's Chip?" asked Fred. He looked suspicious. He didn't know Chip, but something told him he *wasn't* going to like the guy.

"He's a wonderful, successful man who's simply been *lost* without Wilma." Pearl turned to Wilma. "I wouldn't have *dreamed* of denying you two the chance for a reunion."

"A reunion?" Fred narrowed his eyes.

"We used to date," Wilma explained. "*Used* to, mother," she added, glaring at Pearl.

By then, Chip had arrived. He bent to kiss Wilma's hand. "Wilma, you look lovelier than ever," he said.

Wilma pulled her hand back. Fred took a step forward, looking as if he'd like to do something awful to Chip.

Chip looked up at Fred. "Oh, I see you've brought a . . ." He couldn't seem to find the word to describe Fred.

"Date," Fred said flatly, still glaring at this new rival.

Pearl just shook her head. Then she grabbed Wilma's arm. "Oh, look, dear," she said. "The Rathbones just arrived. Let's go say hello, shall we?" She pulled Wilma away.

That left Chip and Fred alone.

"We haven't been formally introduced," said Chip. "I'm Chip Rockefeller, of the Mesozoic Rockefellers." He stuck out a hand, and they shook.

Fred grabbed a snack off a passing tray. "I'm Fred Flintstone," he said. "Of the . . . Fredizoic Flintstones." He took a bite of the cracker and it crumbled all down his shirt. He tried to brush it off.

Chip just stood there, smirking. "Tell me, Flintstone, what line of work are you in?"

Fred stood up straighter and puffed out his chest. "Well, it just so happens I'll be hanging my hat down at the quarry," he said proudly. He was still feeling pretty good about passing his exam.

"Oh, you *bought* Slate and Company?" Chip looked impressed.

"No, I'm a bronto crane operator." Fred had slumped just a little.

Chip chuckled. "No, seriously. What do you do?"

Fred looked confused. "I work at the quarry," he repeated. "I'm a brontocrane operator."

Chip stared at him. Then he began to laugh for real. "You're actually serious!" he said, between guffaws. "Oh, how embarrassing for you!"

Fred looked as if he'd like to disappear. He felt about two inches high.

"Fellas," cried Chip, walking off to join his friends. "Get this! Wilma's 'date' works at the quarry!"

It seemed as if everybody at the party was laughing at Fred. I felt sorry for him, but . . . not too! I couldn't resist rubbing it in, just a little. I popped into Fred's line of vision. "I'm confused," I said. "Why would a woman break up with *him* to go out with you?"

Fred thought hard. "Well, you know," he said finally. "He . . . I mean I'm . . . and he's . . ."

"He's wealthier than you are," I said, ticking off items on one hand.

"Yes, but . . ."

"And handsome."

"Well, that's a matter of taste," said Fred.

"More intelligent than you," I went on. I knew it was mean, but I couldn't help myself.

"I don't know about that," countered Fred.

"You don't?" I asked.

"Hey!" said Fred. "If that Rockefeller guy is so great, why did Wilma break up with him? Hmmm?"

"Who said *she* broke up with *him*?" I asked, just to make trouble.

Meanwhile, over by the patio, Betty was standing all alone, looking uncomfortable. Wilma walked up to her, a little uncertain.

"Hi, Betty," she said tentatively. "I love that dress on you."

"Thank you," answered Betty coolly.

"You're not still mad at me, are you?" asked Wilma.

"Mad?" Betty glared at her. "Why should I be mad? Because you pretended to be poor and I took you in and felt sorry for you and fed you and took care of you so I could come here and be stared at by your *real* friends, 'Tippy' and 'Gippy,' like I was something that just crawled out of the primordial ooze? Why should that make me mad?" She stomped off.

Wilma didn't know what to do. Betty was right.

Wilma went to find her father. Maybe he could make her feel better. She searched through the mansion until she found him on the balcony overlooking Bedrock, the same balcony she'd spent so much time on before she ran away.

"Having fun, princess?" asked the Colonel.

"Not really, Daddy." Wilma couldn't help being honest.

"That's my girl," said the Colonel, as if he hadn't heard. "Here. I got you a little something for your birthday."

"Daddy, it's *your* birthday."

"It is?" He looked shocked. "Oh. Well, these wouldn't fit me, so why don't you take them?" He handed Wilma a box.

She opened it to find a glittering strand of huge white rock pearls. "Oh! They're beautiful!"

"I know you don't like showy things," said the Colonel, "but they were your great-great-grandmother's. In fact, they came right out of her shell."

"Thank you," said Wilma, smiling up at him.

"Wilma," said the Colonel, "I want you to know that no matter what you do or who you decide to be with, I'll still love you."

Wilma gave her father a huge hug. "Thanks, Daddy," she said, tears in her eyes.

CHAPTER EIGHT
Party On!

Wilma was wearing the pearls the next time Fred saw her. That was when she sat down next to him at the long, long dinner table inside the huge Slaghoople dining room. All the other guests were already seated. Pearl was sitting on Fred's right, while Wilma was on his left.

Since Fred didn't want to look at Pearl, who was glaring at him, he turned to Wilma. "Wow, Wilma, those sure are beautiful pearls. They look really . . . expensive."

"Oh, now *that's* tacky," Pearl muttered.

Fred blushed. He couldn't say anything right.

Just then, Chip stood up. "Everyone, I'd like to propose a toast," he said smoothly, smiling around at all the guests. "To the Colonel on his birthday. He's a man of great wealth and property, but he has the most priceless gifts any man could ever want. A loving wife — and the most beautiful daughter the world has ever seen."

Everyone clinked their glasses. "To the Colonel!" they said.

Pearl smiled adoringly at Chip.

Wilma looked uncomfortable.

The Colonel just splashed his spoon in his soup.

Then Fred stood up. (I have to hand it to him. The boy is brave.) "You know," he announced, "I'd also like to propose a toast."

"Oh, Fred," Wilma murmured lovingly.

"Must you?" Pearl sniped at Fred.

Fred cleared his throat. "To Mr. Slag-hoople . . ."

"*Colonel* Slaghoople," Chip corrected him.

"Yes?" asked the Colonel, snapping to attention.

Fred just plowed ahead. "And Mrs. Slaghoople, and most of all Wilma. Thanks for the invite. I've never been to a place this big without paying admission first." He laughed a little, to show that it was a joke. Nobody else laughed. Fred wondered, Were rich people born without funny bones?

Fred went on. "At first, I felt out of place here. Much the same way you would if you stumbled into one of my lodge meetings . . ." He stuck out his chest proudly. "I belong to the loyal order of the Water Buffalos."

He looked down the table at Barney, and both of them made antlers with their hands.

"Waka Waka Wee!" they shouted together, bonded in Water Buffalo brotherhood.

Pearl looked horrified. The guests tittered.

"But the way I figure it," Fred continued, "people is people and the only difference between us is the company we keep . . ."

Suddenly he was interrupted by a huge crash. The double doors at one end of the dining room flew open, and — guess who's coming to dinner? — *Dino* came bounding in, still dragging the tree behind him. He headed straight for the table — and Fred.

"Dino?" Fred couldn't believe his eyes.

Dino just kept on coming.

"No! No! Bad!" Fred shouted. How could this be happening? "Dino, sit!"

"Secure the beach!" shouted the Colonel, springing into action.

Dino hopped right up onto the table and ran across it at full speed, right toward his beloved Fred. The tree dragged along behind him, knocking plates and glasses and silverware off the table. Suddenly, the Slaghoople dining room looked like the scene of a huge food fight. Every single guest was covered with mounds of dripping, oozing food.

Dino didn't stop until he'd reached Fred. When he got there, he knocked Fred to the floor and started licking his face wildly. But the tree had momentum. It kept going, whipping along toward the end of the table, knocking things off right and left. A bowl of soup flew high into the air and landed upside down — right on Pearl's head. Noodles and soup streamed down her face.

"That's it!" she cried. "You've ruined my entire party, you buffoon, you idiot, you . . . commoner!"

Fred tried to shove Dino off him. He was mortified.

"GET OUT!" yelled Pearl.

A team of waiters moved toward Fred, who now had Dino in a hammerlock.

Barney kept eating. He'd never seen such good food, even if it was a little mushed up. He didn't even realize he was about to be kicked out of the mansion along with Fred.

"Mother!" cried Wilma. "How dare you treat people this way just because they're not like you!" She stood up, hands on hips. "Well, that's why I like them — because they're not like you. They like me for who I am, not for who I am. I mean . . . *you* know what I mean!"

Pearl's face turned red, then white. "No one's ever spoken to me in that tone."

"Well, then, it's about time someone did! Happy Birthday, Daddy. Good-bye, Mother."

"We're right behind you, Wilma," said Betty. She and Wilma smiled at each other.

Wilma grabbed Fred and marched out. Betty grabbed Barney, too. A little reluctantly, he put down his fork. Then he turned to Pearl. "You can just kiss your invitation to the Water Buffalo pancake breakfast good-bye!" he told her. He and Betty tossed their heads as they marched out behind Fred and Wilma.

Shoulders straight, the foursome swept out of the huge, heavy main doors of the mansion, with

Dino trotting along behind them. But before Fred could tell the valet to fetch his car, Chip came running out.

"Wilma! Wait, wait, don't go. You were right back there. The way everyone's behaved today has been just inexcusable."

"Thank you, Chip," said Wilma, a little uncertainly. Could he possibly be — sincere?

Chip put out his hand to Fred. "Congratulations, Flintstone. I mean that. I'm willing to admit that the better man won. And, just to show you there are no hard feelings, I'd like to invite all four of you to the opening of my newest casino in Rock Vegas."

Betty gasped.

Chip went on, smiling. "You lovebirds can take in the sights, relax in the luxury accommodations, and then enjoy the opening night gala concert." He paused dramatically. "Our main act will be Mick Jagged and the Stones."

"The Stones?" Barney looked excited. "I *love* the Stones."

"Ooh," squealed Betty. "Me, too!"

"So, what do you say?" Chip looked at Wilma.

Wilma didn't answer right away. She didn't trust Chip at all, and something told her he wasn't inviting them out of the goodness of his heart. "I appreciate the gesture, Chip," she said slowly, "but I'm not sure . . ."

"Rock Vegas, eh?" asked Fred. I could almost see his thoughts. If he could win lots of clams at the slot machines, he'd be able to afford a huge engagement ring for Wilma. "We'd love to go!" he said.

CHAPTER NINE
Viva Rock Vegas!

A few days later, Fred and Wilma and Barney and Betty climbed aboard Chip's private jet. They took their seats in a luxurious cabin on top of the hugest pterodactyl I've ever seen. Soon, the dinosaur ran down the runway and took off, its huge wings flapping majestically as it rose into the sky.

Watching, I shook my head. I didn't trust Chip anymore than Wilma did. I knew he must have his own reasons for inviting Wilma and her friends to Rock Vegas. And — I hated to admit it, but I was beginning to be just a tad fond of the four of them. I decided it was time for me to take a little Vegas vacation of my own.

*　　*　　*

Fred had left Dino in a brand new pen, set up near the gaping hole where the tree used to be. "This time, he's gonna stay put," he'd told Barney. Now, as Chip's jet flapped overhead, Dino sat up and took notice. As the plane flew by, he began to bark — softly at first, and then louder and louder. He ran up and down in the pen, frantic to get to Fred. Finally, he began to dig. Dino dug as fast as he could, scrabbling into the dirt and leaving huge piles behind him. Within moments, he was free. He ran along, watching the plane and whimpering. He jumped — and jumped again. Poor Dino. He had no idea how high that plane really was. He kept leaping and jumping, until finally one jump landed him right into the back of a parked truck. He tumbled inside, just as the driver came around to close the back gate. Then the driver headed back to the cab, started up the truck, and drove off, never noticing his new cargo.

There was a big sign on the side of the truck. O'CARNIVORE AND SONS MEAT DELIVERY, it blared in giant writing. WE'RE THE KING OF BRONTO STEAKS!

The truck trundled on down the highway, passing a road sign that read ROCK VEGAS: REALLY, REALLY FAR AWAY. Dino was on his way.

*   *   *

"Wow!" cried Betty as the plane began its descent toward the lights of Vegas. "Isn't it beautiful?"

Once they'd landed, they rented the biggest convertible they could find, a Cadi-Roc El Dorocko. "Always wanted to drive one of these babies," said Fred, climbing behind the wheel.

As they drove into town, past the sign that said WELCOME TO ROCK VEGAS, they whooped and hollered. They cruised down the main street (Fred said it was known as "the strip"), looking at all the brightly lit signs that advertised upcoming shows. FRANK STONEATRA! CHRIS ROCK — IN CONCERT! CIRQUE DE SOIL! SLIME AND THE FAMILY STONE! The signs blinked on and off, creating a dazzling display.

Finally, Fred pulled up in front of the Tardust Hotel, which Chip owned. This time, he knew enough to toss the keys to the valet standing by. Then, he and Wilma and Barney and Betty walked inside.

"Holy mastodons!" said Barney. "Would you look at this place?" He gazed around, awestruck by the fancy furnishings in the gigantic lobby.

He was even more impressed when they ar-

62

rived in their rooms. Chip had booked them into a whole suite of interconnected rooms: a bedroom for Betty and Wilma, a bedroom for Fred and Barney, plus a huge whirlpool Jacuzzi in a sunken living room overlooking the lights of the strip. "Check out this entertainment system," Fred said, looking at the wall full of equipment. "Barn? Check this out."

But Barney didn't hear him. He was already in the Jacuzzi.

The next day, after a huge breakfast, the gang spent hours lounging around the pool. Every time Fred did a cannonball, the elephants who filled the pool had to work extra hard to replace the water he'd splashed out of it. They looked pretty tired by the time darkness fell.

That's when the live band began to play, right out there by the pool, and Fred asked Wilma to dance. They looked so happy together, dancing cheek-to-cheek.

"Great day, huh?" Fred spoke softly into Wilma's ear as they twirled around.

"I hope it never ends," Wilma answered, smiling up at him.

CHAPTER TEN
Rocko and Rocko

Chip laughed an evil laugh and turned to his assistant, a beautiful showgirl named Roxie. She was doing her nails, and not paying much attention at all to Chip.

"Hmm?" she asked vaguely.

"He's so naive, this flat-footed Flintstone," Chip went on. He pressed the remote control he was holding, and a little bird flew out to shut off the monitor. When it had done its job, it flew back into the remote.

"Hmmm," Roxie murmured again.

"Just you watch, Roxie my dear. This man is my puppet, and I've barely begun to pull the strings. Soon Wilma will see him for the pathetic, primitive primate that he is." Chip was practically rubbing his hands with glee.

Finally Roxie took notice. "I thought you said you were over that Wilma person," she said, pouting a little.

"Oh, dear Roxie," said Chip. "Do you honestly think I could prefer that plain Jane to you? What do I have to give you to prove how much I care? Do you want diamonds? A fancy car like a Maserocki? Your own show in the Stalactite Lounge?"

Roxie yawned. "Actually," she said. "I prefer cash."

"What a coincidence. So do we."

Chip whirled around to see where the gruff male voice was coming from. Two big men stood looming in the doorway.

"Ah," said Chip smoothly, trying not to show how alarmed he was. "Rocko and Rocko. What can I do for you 'gentlemen'?"

"Our boss wants the money you owe him," said one of the Rockos, the one who was just slightly smaller. "The money he lent you to build this fancy hotel."

"He says you better get it to him by midnight Sunday, or he'll start taking away your hotels and casinos," said the other one, Big Rocko.

"Not only that," added Little Rocko. "He says he might have to tip off the Feds to the funny way you've been keeping your books. You could be in a lot of trouble if they find out you haven't been paying all your taxes, with all the money you make."

"No problem, no problem," Chip assured them, holding up both hands. "We don't even need to have this discussion, gentlemen. See, by Sunday night, I will be married to Wilma Slaghoople, heiress to one of the greatest personal fortunes in the uncivilized world."

"You better be," said Little Rocko.

"Or else," echoed Big Rocko.

They both pointed at Chip, giving him threatening looks. Then they turned and left.

Chip, usually so suave, looked slightly nervous. Me? I was shaking. I'd been watching from a corner near the ceiling the whole time, and I have to tell you, those Rockos made my blood run cold. Of course, since I'm an alien, it runs cold most of the time. But you know what I mean. I didn't want to get on the wrong side of those big boys. Not that I'd want Chip as an enemy either. I didn't envy Fred at all.

And Wilma? Poor Wilma had no idea what Chip was planning for her. She and Betty spent most of the next day relaxing in the hotel's spa. I peeked in as they were getting a massage.

They lay on comfy couches, wrapped in thick white towels. One giant octopus massaged both of them, reaching tentacles across to rub their backs and shoulders.

"Mmm," said Betty. She looked adorable in her heart-shaped sunglasses. "This is heaven."

Wilma spoke to the octopus. "Could you get right between my shoulders?" she asked. "That's where I store all my tension."

The octopus looked up at me and raised its eyebrows. "*She's* tense? I just found out what 'calamari' means."

Quickly, I checked my internal translator and learned that calamari is Italian for cooked octopus. I gave the masseuse a sympathetic look.

Betty sighed with contentment. "Wilma," she said, "can I ask you something?"

"Sure, Betty."

"Do you think Barney's serious about me?"

"What are you talking about?" asked Wilma. "Of course he is. He's crazy about you."

"I hope so." Betty sighed again. "I've never met anyone like Bernard Rubble. He's so loyal, so sweet. He just makes me feel like I'm the only girl in this whole, flat world."

Wilma smiled at her. "Fred makes me feel the same way. He's so different from all my former suitors. I mean, Chip? All he ever wanted to talk about was buying land or trading stegosaurus bellies. It was always about money. But Fred doesn't have a greedy bone in his body."

Sweet, sweet Wilma. Little did she know.

CHAPTER ELEVEN
Fred on a Roll

"Yabba Dabba Dough!"

That was Fred, jumping for joy as the man in the tuxedo announced that he had won again. He was feeling good — no, he was feeling *great*. In fact, he'd never felt better.

Fred was rolling dice at a table in the casino, betting all his money and — surprisingly — winning. He had a huge pile of clams in front of him, and a big crowd of people had gathered to watch. He raked another pile toward him just as Barney came up next to him. "Look at all these clams, Barn!" he exclaimed.

"Great, Fred," said his friend. "You've got enough to buy Wilma a ring for each finger. And maybe a little bauble for me, too. Why don't we go cash in your clams?"

"What, are you crazy?" Fred stared at Barney. Then he shook his head, pityingly. "That's your problem, Barn. You think too small. I'm not gonna stop at some measly ring. I'm gonna win enough clams to buy Wilma a whole lifestyle, just like Chip Rockefeller's!"

"But Fred," Barney pleaded. "She doesn't want a rich, handsome guy. She wants you."

A woman elbowed Barney aside. "Buzz off, little man," she said. "This guy's winning for all of us. We don't want him to stop." The rest of the crowd nodded in agreement.

"That's right," said Fred. "Thank you for your advice, Barney, but I think I know better." He picked up the dice and got ready to roll again.

That's when I entered, stage left. I spoke into Fred's ear.

"I know this might be difficult for you to follow," I began, "but let's just think for a moment. Chip Rockefeller flew you to *his* casino, in *his* plane, to gamble at *his* dice table. The odds of winning this game are about, oh, two hundred and forty-seven thousand to one. And you've just rolled seventeen straight winners. Can we connect the dots?" I couldn't have spelled it out any more clearly.

"Sure," Fred said, with a huge smile. "Today's my lucky day!" He shook the dice. "C'mon, seven!" he cried, throwing them down on the table.

"Lllllucky seven!" called out the man in the tuxedo. "We have another winner!"

The crowd around the table burst into cheers. Fred beamed.

"Well," I said. "I did my best. I'm out of here." I couldn't watch anymore. It was obvious to me that Chip was setting Fred up, but if Fred wouldn't listen to reason, what could I do?

Fred ignored me. He was too busy scooping up the huge pile of clams he'd just won. "What'd I tell you, Barn?" he asked his friend. "Magic!"

Just then, Chip Rockefeller appeared, gliding up to the table. He winked at the man in the tuxedo, then turned to Fred. "It's not magic, my friend. It's skill. You know, a gentleman gambler like you should be playing with the high rollers." He nodded toward a roped-off section of the floor.

Fred's eyes lit up. "Really?" he asked. Ha.

Unlike Barney, Chip obviously knew a winner when he saw one.

Chip led him over to the area. "This is where you belong," he said, waving a hand toward the cluster of well-dressed, obviously very wealthy and powerful people playing there.

"With the high rollers?" Fred asked again. He was flattered by Chip's attention, but he wasn't so sure he belonged with all those sleek men and women in their tuxedos and long, glittery gowns. "Well, I — uh — I was really just getting warmed up. You know, building my bankroll."

"Bankroll?" Chip asked, waving a hand dismissively. "Please. I'll give you a line of credit."

"Credit?" Fred frowned. He wasn't familiar with all these gambling terms.

"Sure! It's simple. The casino gives you a little money up front, and then you give it right back after you've won more. A man with your skill *deserves* a house account. Please, it would be an honor."

Barney tugged on Fred's sleeve. "Fred, no!" he hissed. "That's how my uncle, the gambler, lost everything. His house, his wife, his job . . ."

Chip turned to Barney. He was annoyed,

and he wanted to shut him up as quickly as possible. He remembered the way Barney had chowed down at the Colonel's birthday party. He forced himself to smile at Barney. "Hey, did you know we have an all-you-can-eat buffet by the pool?"

Barney forgot all about warning Fred. "*All* you can eat?" he asked Chip. Suddenly, he looked like a dog about to get a biscuit. I wouldn't have been surprised to see him roll over and offer to shake hands.

"Absolutely."

"Is there a shortcut to the pool?"

Chip smiled. "Roxie!" he called, waving his assistant over. "Would you kindly show Mr. Rubble to the buffet?"

"It would bring me great pleasure," said Roxie, stepping up to take Barney's arm in hers. Her slinky dress sparkled as she moved.

Barney was in heaven. A beautiful hostess, a buffet full of food . . . He walked off without a second glance at Fred.

Now Chip and Fred were alone again. "C'mon, Flintstone," said Chip, "let me show you to your table. And I'll have one of my helpers bring you a nice, big pile of clams."

Barefoot in Bedrock: Fred Flintstone and
Wilma Slaghoople are made for each other.

A perfect prehistoric pair:
Barney Rubble and Betty O'Shale.

Rich and snobby Chip Rockefeller wants to marry Wilma—but does he love her? Nuh-*uh!*

The fastest way to Barney's heart is through his stomach.

Fred is a simple guy—all he can give Wilma is lots of love. But that's all she needs.

Fred "wins" baby Dino for Wilma at a carnival—and Dino is a handful of mischief!

Bright lights, big city: Fred, Wilma, Betty, and Barney take in the sights of Rock Vegas.

Betty and Wilma get pampered with an octopus massage!

Mick Jagged and the Stones
rock the house . . .

. . . as the Flintstones and pals
shake their bonbons!

Mr. & Mrs. Flintstone . . .
and they lived happily ever after!

Before Fred knew it, he was seated at a table full of very sophisticated gamblers, playing cards. He could barely see over the pile of clams Chip had placed in front of him, and he still wasn't sure he belonged there. But Fred was happy. Why? Because his good luck was holding.

"Read 'em and weep," he said, laying down a hand of cards for everyone to see. "Four lovely ladies." (I found out later that meant he had four queens.)

"Fred!"

He turned to see Wilma and Betty walking up to his table. "Make that six," he cracked. "Where have you two been?"

"At the Kavern Klub. Waiting for you." Wilma looked annoyed. Fred had totally forgotten their plans.

"Oh, right," said Fred. "Sorry, Wilma, I've been on a roll. I can't stop now. I'll catch up with you later." He was already watching the dealer deal a new hand of cards. Fred had caught the gambling bug, big time.

Wilma stared at him in disbelief.

Meanwhile, Betty was looking around. "Hey, where's Barney?" she asked.

"Oh, he went off to the buffet a while ago," answered Fred, barely looking up from the table.

Betty looked relieved. But Wilma was still ticked off at Fred. "You mean you just left him?" she asked.

"No, no," said Fred, barely paying attention. "He left *me*. He went off with some babe."

"What?" Betty stomped off to look for Barney.

Fred shrugged and went back to the game. Without even picking up his cards, he said, "I bet you a grand, raise you five grand, and I haven't even seen my cards yet!" He was showing off for Wilma, but she was not impressed.

Meanwhile, out by the buffet, Barney couldn't have been happier. He was strolling around, filling his plate with a little of every delicacy he came across, and a lot of some of them. He looked perfectly content, as happy as a mastodon in a mudhole.

Roxie looked bored.

"You know," she told him, "when they say 'all you can eat' they don't mean 'til you explode.' "

"Hmm?" Barney's mouth was full. "Oh, I haven't even gotten started yet. Ooh! Look at the size of those pies!" A waiter was walking by with a tray stacked high with huge, fluffy cream pies. "Waiter, over here!" called Barney.

"Why don't you let me . . ." Roxie began, but it was too late. The waiter spun around and several pies flew off the tray — straight into Roxie's face!

"Thanks," she said, wiping off some of the cream. "I always wanted to be in vaudeville."

The waiter was apologetic. "I'm so sorry, miss. I'll be right back to clean this up." He scurried off.

Barney was apologetic, too. "I'm sorry, Roxie. Let me help." He put down his plate and grabbed some napkins. Then he started wiping cream off Roxie.

Just then, Betty appeared in the doorway. Barney had his back to her, so he didn't notice her arrival. But she definitely noticed what he was doing. To her, it looked as if Barney was hugging Roxie.

Betty was horrified. Her face fell, and tears came to her eyes. So much for her loyal, loving Barney. How could she have been so trusting? She ran off before Barney even turned around.

CHAPTER TWELVE
In the Mick of Time

Betty ran straight outside to the pool and collapsed on the edge of a beautiful fountain, holding her face in her hands. Dusk was gathering, and she was glad. That meant nobody would see her crying.

Nobody, that is, but Mick Jagged — the rock star.

"Hello, luv," he said, in his very British accent.

"Are you —?" Betty couldn't believe her eyes.

Mick bowed. As he rose up, he took Betty's hand and kissed it. "Mick Jagged, at your service," he said gallantly. "And you are?"

"Betty." She sniffled a little. "Betty O'Shale."

"Tell me, Miss Betty O'Shale. What's a lovely bird like you doing out here all by your lonesome?" Mick looked concerned, caring.

"My boyfriend, he was . . . I saw him —" Betty couldn't help herself. She burst into tears all over again. "I saw him with another girl!" she finally finished.

"Oh, sweetheart." Mick sat a little closer. "I'll tell you wot. If you were my lady, I wouldn't even look at another girl. Not ever."

Betty cried even harder.

"Hey, now," he said, "why don't you stop crying and give Mick a little smile, eh?"

Betty sniffled again. Mick reached out to wipe away her tears. Betty gave him a tiny smile.

"There. That's better. You are lovely when you smile, Miss Betty O'Shale."

Betty blushed and looked down at her hands. Was it really possible that *the* Mick Jagged was talking to her this way? "Thank you," she managed to choke out.

He smiled at her tenderly. "Would you like to meet my bandmates?" he asked.

*   *   *

Later that evening, Fred and Wilma were dining at the Kavern Klub, in a luxury booth overlooking the hotel's grand lobby. Fred had spent the entire afternoon in the high rollers area, and his success there had definitely gone to his head. He was surrounded by buckets of clams, and he was out to make the most of his winnings. He'd make Chip Rockefeller look like a little boy with a tiny allowance.

"Miss!" he called, snapping his fingers. "Over here, Miss!"

Wilma cringed, embarrassed at the way Fred was bossing the waitresses around.

"Bring me a bottle of your best bubbly! And let's have some of that cave-iar!"

"Have you ever tasted cave-iar, Fred?" asked Wilma. "Actually, do you even know what it is?"

"Nope," admitted Fred. "But it's gotta be good. Look how much it costs!"

Wilma sighed. "But Fred, I don't even like —"

Just then, a flower vendor strolled by, carrying buckets full of huge, prehistoric flowers. "Flower for the lady?"

"Absolutely!" Fred shoved a pile of clams

toward the vendor and took all of the flowers. They were so big and showy that they created sort of a forest on the table. Wilma disappeared behind it.

Fred didn't seem to notice. "Nothing's too good for my girl!" he boasted. He looked up to see Barney walking by. "Hey, Barn!" he called. "Over here!"

"Hey, Fred," said Barney, taking a seat. "Where are the girls?"

"I'm right here," said Wilma, from behind the flowers.

"Oh." Barney looked confused. "Is Betty in there with you?"

"No." Wilma didn't seem to want to talk, so Barney turned his attention to the cave-iar the waiter had just delivered.

"This looks interesting," he said. He hadn't had his fill at the buffet.

"Have all you want." Fred barely noticed. He was counting his clams for the twentieth time. "Three thousand forty-one," he said, "three thousand forty-two . . ."

Just then, there was a huge commotion in the lobby below.

"What's going on down there?" asked Fred.

"Great, now I've lost count!" He went back to the first bucket and started all over again. "One, two, three . . ."

"Fred!" cried Barney. "Look! It's Mick Jagged and the Stones!"

The rockers crossed the lobby, with hordes of screaming fans following their every move.

Suddenly, Barney's eyes grew wide. "Look who's with them!" He jumped up to get a better view. "It's Betty! She's with the band!"

"Don't be silly, Barney," said Wilma, shoving the flowers aside so she could see. "What would Betty be doing with the band?"

"Yeah," said Fred. "She doesn't even play an instrument."

Barney didn't listen. He ran down to the top of the stairs and yelled down to Betty. "Hey, Betty! Over here! It's me, Barney!"

But Betty couldn't hear him over the shrieks of the adoring fans. Barney ran down the stairs as fast as he could and tried to push through the crowds to Betty. But just as the band — and Betty — entered the elevator, a couple of burly security guards grabbed Barney.

"Wait!" He struggled to get out of their grasp. "I gotta see them!"

"Then buy a ticket," barked one of the guards, as they tossed Barney out of the lobby.

Upstairs, Fred didn't even notice what was happening. He was still too busy counting his clams. "Fourteen thousand five hundred and forty-two, *fifteen* thousand and forty-two! Look at this! I'm up over fifteen thousand clams!"

Wilma just shook her head. Money didn't impress her. She wanted her old Fred back. "Come on, Fred," she said. "Let's do something together. We could . . . go bowling!"

"Bowling? Bowling's for poor people."

Wilma just looked at him. "You know, Fred? Maybe you and Chip have more in common than I thought."

"Why?" asked Fred, innocently. "Because we're both big winners?" He gestured around at all his clams.

Wilma stood up, reached into her pocket book, and tossed Fred a clam. "Here, Fred," she said quietly. "Buy yourself a clue."

Then she turned and left. Fred sat there

looking stunned for a second. Then he jumped to his feet and ran after her.

"Wilma! Wilma!" He chased her into the casino. "Wait, Wilma! What's the matter?" He ran past a row of slot machines — and suddenly put on the brakes. He looked ahead to see Wilma getting into an elevator. Then he looked back at the slot machines. It was as if they had some magnetic attraction.

He drifted back to one the machines, pulled out a clam, and started to pull the handle.

CHAPTER THIRTEEN
Sometimes You Win, Sometimes You Lose

Way up above, in his offices in the hotel, Chip Rockefeller was watching on the monitors. So far, everything was going according to plan. "All right, Flintstone," he snickered. "You've lost Wilma. Now it's time to lose everything else." He walked over to a huge control panel. One of the levers, made out of a huge wishbone, was marked SLOT MACHINE. Chip flipped it from WIN to LOSE.

Then he walked out of the room, took an elevator to the lobby, and arranged himself at the desk just in time for Wilma to walk by.

"Hello, Wilma," he said. "Taking a walk?"

"Nothing gets by you, Chip," Wilma commented sarcastically.

Chip looked hurt. "Oh. Forgive me for disturbing you."

"Look, Chip, I'm sorry. I've just . . . I've got a lot on my mind." Wilma seemed very distracted. She couldn't understand why Fred was acting so strangely.

"I've been on edge myself," Chip told her. "You know. Opening weekend, the Stones, all these guests, and now all these room robberies . . ." He stopped suddenly and covered his mouth.

"Robberies?" asked Wilma, suddenly frightened.

"It's nothing," said Chip. "It's just, well, even with all the security we have . . . it's nothing to worry about, really. Believe me, we're on top of it." He paused. "But just to be safe, I wish you'd let me put those beautiful pearls of yours in the office safe."

Wilma looked down at the pearls the Colonel had given her. She hadn't taken them off since the night he'd fastened them around her neck. "That's very thoughtful, Chip." She turned around so he could undo the clasp.

Chip took off the pearls and placed them carefully into the big stone safe behind the desk.

Then he locked the safe. "Wilma," he said, standing up and looking deeply into her eyes. "I want you to know, I'm still your friend. So if you ever want to talk, or . . ."

"Oh, no," Wilma interrupted. "I'll be fine. I think I'll just go to bed now." She drifted off.

Chip watched her go. Then he looked down at the safe and smiled a very nasty smile.

CHAPTER FOURTEEN
Fred's Good Luck Runs Out

Down in the casino, suddenly, Fred couldn't do anything right. He'd lost several buckets of clams at the slot machines, and now he was playing poker.

"Read 'em and weep," said Fred, putting down his hand for everyone to see.

One of the other players put down a better hand.

Fred started to cry.

Then he tried the roulette wheel. He put down a bet, and an octopus spun the wheel. When the wheel came to a stop, Fred had lost again. He frowned as the octopus pulled away yet another big pile of his clams.

The dice table was no better. Fred couldn't roll a lucky seven for anything.

Finally, he went back to the slot machines with his last few buckets of clams. He got five machines going at once, but no winners were coming up. He tried again, with five *other* machines. No luck. And again. Still, no luck.

Just then, Barney came up to him. "Fred, can I talk to you for a sec?"

"Aw, Barn," said Fred, as he lost again. "You just jinxed me." He shoved Barney out of the way so he could pull the arm of the slot machine again.

"But Fred," pleaded Barney. "It's about Betty. She's hanging out with Mick Jagged. She wouldn't even look at me. I think she's mad about something. Maybe you could go explain to her —"

Fred pushed Barney out of the way again. "Sure, sure," he mumbled.

Barney was relieved. "So, could you do it now?" he asked.

"Do what?"

"Talk to Betty!"

"About what?" asked Fred, distracted and

impatient. "Look, Barney, can we talk about this when I'm richer?"

Barney looked very hurt. "Sure, Fred. If that's the way you want it." He shuffled off.

I couldn't stand it another minute. I popped into Fred's view. "Way to go, dum-dum," I said. (I know, I promised I'd stop calling him that. But under the circumstances, can you blame me?) "Let's see. You've lost Wilma, you've lost your best friend, in fact, you've lost just about everything but that extra five pounds around your waist."

"Oh, yeah?" Fred asked. "Well, I've had just about enough of you! So why don't you go back to the other side of the universe, and take that over-sized head of yours with you."

Well! "Oversized head? Now, look here," I said, "I'm just here to observe. There's no need to get personal."

"Personal?" asked Fred. "I was just observing *you*, and guess what? Your nose is too big for your face."

Ouch. That stung. "I was born this way," I said. What was I doing? After all, I am a superior being. I didn't have to stay there and trade witticisms with a man that evolution apparently forgot.

"Good luck, dum-dum. You'll need it." With that, I took off.

Fred didn't seem to care. He reached into his bucket and pulled out his very last clam.

"C'mon, baby," he said, kissing it for good luck, "it's up to you! Get me started again." He started to put it into the slot, but he fumbled and dropped it onto the floor. Just then, a janitor passed by with a vacuum cleaner.

Fred's last clam disappeared straight up the hose.

"Nooo!" Fred howled.

He ran after the vacuum cleaner — and smack into a human wall made up of two huge security guards.

"Mr. Flintstone," one of them said, "Mr. Rockefeller has extended an invitation to join him at the fights."

"Great!" Fred's face lit up. "I'll ask him for more credit. How can he say no?"

"No." Chip leaned back in his seat. "No way. No how. Do you know how much you owe me already?"

He and Fred were sitting ringside at the boxing match. Two oversized neanderthals were in the ring, grunting and swinging clubs at each other. The crowd was going wild. But Fred had only one thing on his mind. He had to get more money out of Chip, before he lost Wilma for good.

"Owe?" he asked.

"Owe." Chip smiled that nasty smile. "Flintstone, you owe me one million, four hundred thousand clams."

Fred couldn't think of a thing to say. "Oh," he finally squeaked out.

"Do you have any idea what a line of credit is?" asked Chip.

"I guess I do now," Fred answered. He suddenly realized that a lot of the money he'd lost wasn't his to begin with. Fred was in big trouble.

"So, Freddie," Chip leaned back again, "how do you plan on settling your account?"

"Well, uh, let's see." Fred thought for a moment. "I figure if I give you a little something outta my paycheck every week, we could be square by, say, the next Ice Age."

Chip shook his head. "Sorry, Flopstone," he said. Then he sighed and made a sad face. "It's going to be a real shame when Wilma finds out what a loser her new boyfriend really is."

Fred slumped in his seat. Wilma. Losing all that money was nothing compared to losing her.

Chip leaned toward him. "Of course," he said, "she doesn't *have* to find out."

"She doesn't?" asked Fred. Suddenly he was full of hope again. "See that? I *knew* you were a nice guy."

"I'm not," answered Chip bluntly. "I said I wouldn't tell her. I didn't say you could still have her. I'll erase your debt, Flintstone, but you've got to disappear. Outta town. Outta Bedrock. And never see or talk to Wilma Slaghoople again."

Fred couldn't believe what Chip was saying. All along, he'd trusted him. Now it was as if a light-bulb went on in Fred's brain. "Wait a minute!" he cried. "You — you had this planned all along! You *wanted* me to lose. That's why you gave me the credit in the first place!"

Chip was amazed that Fred was just catching on. "Tell me, Flintstone, how do you even dress yourself in the morning?"

Fred pondered this. "Well, usually I just

wear whatever I fell asleep in," he answered. "But what's *that* got to do with anything?"

Chip just shook his head. "Good-bye, Flint-stone," he said, laughing as he got up and walked away.

"Hey!" cried Fred.

Just then, one of the neanderthals gave a huge heave and threw the other one out of the ring. He landed right on top of Fred. That was the last straw.

Fred got up and shook himself. Then he took off after Chip. He caught up with him in the lobby. "You know what?" he asked, stepping right up to Chip. "I don't care what happens to me. But I'm not gonna let you weasel your way closer to Wilma! As soon as I find her I'm gonna tell her exactly what's going on! Then we'll see how well your plan worked." He folded his arms and stared at Chip.

Chip stared back. Then he smiled. He gestured to a security guard, who reached over to pull a feather and set off the alarm bird system. The bird started squawking.

"What — ?" Fred panicked.

A set of gates crashed down at each of the doors, closing off all the exits.

"What's going on?" Fred asked. Something was happening, and it didn't feel right.

"Uh-oh," Chip answered. "It appears there's been a robbery. Looks like we'll have to continue this conversation later, Fred. Please, step this way." He took Fred's arm to guide him across the lobby.

As they walked, he reached over carefully and slipped Wilma's pearls right into Fred's pocket. Fred didn't notice a thing.

CHAPTER FIFTEEN
A Thief Revealed

The alarm birds flew all over the hotel, squawking loudly. Guests began to pour into the lobby. Some were in their pajamas, some were still dressed in tuxedos, and some were only wrapped in towels, as if they'd just gotten out of their Jacuzzis.

Barney stumbled in, rubbing his eyes. Betty and Wilma appeared also, standing by the elevators near Mick Jagged and the rest of the Stones.

Fred just stood there, looking bewildered.

Then Chip picked up a microphone. "Ladies and gentlemen," he announced. "I regret to inform you that there is a criminal in our midst."

"Oooh!" the crowd murmured. Everybody started talking at once.

Chip held up his hand for silence. "Now, this person knows who he is, and he knows the horribly heinous deed he has perpetrated. But before I expose him to the public, I would like to give him the chance to step forward. Step forward and admit his wrongdoing, if only to take the first tiny step towards absolution." Chip fell silent and waited.

The crowd was quiet. People shot nervous glances at their neighbors. The tension grew.

Finally, a man stepped forward. "Fine!" he shouted. "It was me! I cheated on my income taxes!"

The crowd gasped.

Chip just shook his head. "Actually, that's not what I —"

A woman spoke up, interrupting him. "I stole all the towels from my room!" she confessed.

"Well," said Chip, "that *is* illegal, but —"

A man in a tuxedo came to the front. "I'm wearing someone else's underwear!" he said, in a loud, steady voice.

"Ewww!" The crowd was grossed out.

"What?" Chip looked bewildered. The situation was getting out of control. He had to get things back on track. "No, I'm talking about —"

Another man jumped up in the back. "I'm systematically poisoning the dinosaurs' water supply!" he yelled. "In a matter of decades, their entire species will be extinct!"

That gave the crowd a good laugh. Dinosaurs, extinct? Ridiculous.

"I mean it!" cried the man. "Just wait! You'll see . . ."

The crowd just kept on laughing.

A very frustrated Chip spoke into the microphone again. "All right, people, this is obviously going nowhere! I'm talking about a necklace, a very valuable necklace that has been stolen from our hotel safe! A necklace belonging to my dear, dear friend Wilma Slaghoople." He pointed right at Wilma.

Wilma was startled. "My pearls?" she gasped. "They've been stolen?" She began to cry.

Betty leaned over to comfort her.

Fred looked furious. "Wilma's pearls?" he roared. "All right, who did it? So help me, if you don't step forward right now, I will personally punch you in —"

Chip stopped him. "I don't think any violence will be necessary, Flintstone. I happen to know exactly who stole Wilma's pearls." He paused for the full dramatic effect. Then he went on. "It was a desperate man, drowning in gambling debts."

The crowd gasped.

"Lowlife!" Fred growled.

The man in the back of the crowd spoke up again. "Doesn't anyone *care* about this whole dinosaurs-becoming-extinct thing?"

"NO!" roared the crowd.

Chip gestured to Fred. "Fred, would you be so kind as to empty your pockets?"

Fred was completely taken by surprise. "Empty my pockets? You think *I* took Wilma's pearls? That's —"

"Do you have something to hide, Fred?" Chip asked patiently.

"Definitely not!" Fred reached into his pockets. "See for yourself. I'm not a —" He stopped. His face turned white. He pulled his hand out of his pocket, and with it came . . . a string of pearls.

"It's him!"

"He did it!"

"The big thief!"

The crowd went bonkers.

Fred was in shock. "Wait a minute! I didn't take these! Wilma, why would I take your pearls? I don't even have earrings to match!"

Chip ignored his lame joke. "Do you deny that you owe the casino over a million clams, with no way to pay it back?" he asked Fred.

Wilma nearly fainted. "Fred, is that true?" she asked. "Over a million clams?"

"Yes, but —"

Chip didn't give Fred a chance to finish. "Wilma, darling, I am so sorry," he said, putting on a sympathetic look.

Wilma turned and ran out of the lobby.

"Wilma, wait!" yelled Fred. "You can't believe him! He set me up!"

"Security!" shouted Chip. "Take this man to jail!"

The crowd clapped and whistled as Chip took the pearls away from Fred.

Barney stepped forward. "Wait a minute," he said. "You're making a big mistake. Sure, Fred may be a jerk. He may be a moron. He may have a brain the size of a pea —"

"I think they get the point, Barn," Fred said, through gritted teeth.

"The point is that he *couldn't* have taken those pearls. They were in a safe. Fred can't even remember the combination to his bowling locker. That's why he's got it written on his hand. Look!" Barney grabbed Fred's hand and showed it to the audience. Sure enough, there was a series of numbers written on it.

"Aw, now everyone's seen it," complained Fred.

"I'm the one who has to do everything for him," Barney went on. "Crack a safe? Why, Fred couldn't crack a walnut without my help!"

"Why, thank you, Mr. Rubble," said Chip. "Thank you for confessing to being Mr. Flintstone's accomplice!"

"You're welcome," said Barney. Then he realized what Chip had said. "What? Wait!"

But it was too late. The security guards were already putting handcuffs onto Fred and Barney.

"Don't worry boys," said Chip. "Prison shouldn't be too much of a change for you. After all, you're used to eating starchy food and breaking rocks twenty hours a day." He smiled his nastiest smile as the guards led Fred and Barney away.

CHAPTER SIXTEEN
Urp!

The guards marched Fred and Barney out to the strip, where a police car was waiting.

Just as the police car drove off with the boys in the backseat, a truck pulled up to the spot in front of the hotel.

A truck with a sign on it.

A sign that said: O'CARNIVORE AND SONS MEAT DELIVERY.

The driver stepped out of the truck and walked around to the back. He opened the gate, only to see Dino lying there happily, his bulging belly full of every single bronto steak the truck had been carrying.

"What the — hey, you mutt!" The driver stared at Dino.

Dino stared back. Then he opened his mouth and burped.

"Get outta here!" yelled the driver.

Obediently, Dino got up — not that it was easy — and waddled out of the truck.

Dino had arrived in Rock Vegas.

Now all he had to do was find Fred.

CHAPTER SEVENTEEN
Dino Saves the Day ... Or Not

"C'mon! Don't we even get a phone call? Guard! Guard!" Fred banged on the bars and hollered.

He and Barney were locked in a dusty cell at the police station. There was one guard, a neanderthal, but he ignored Fred and walked out, his arms swinging to the ground.

"Ah, what's the use?" Fred collapsed on a bench. "The only person in the world I could call is Wilma. And she probably won't speak to me ever again."

Barney didn't say a word.

"*You're* not speaking to me either, are you?" Fred knew it was time to apologize. "I'm sorry, Barn."

"For what?" Barney asked. "For getting me locked in jail, or for ignoring me in the casino when I was asking for your help with Betty?"

Fred looked ashamed. "Both, I guess."

Fortunately, Barney wasn't the type to hold a grudge. "That's all right. I know you didn't mean it. And I know you didn't steal that necklace, buddy." He paused and glanced at Fred out of the corners of his eyes. "Did you?"

"Of course not, Barney!" Fred exploded. "Why would I steal Wilma's necklace?"

Barney thought for a second. "I guess you could sell it to buy her a bigger engagement ring," he said.

"Then why wouldn't I just steal a ring?" For once, Fred was being logical.

"You stole a ring, too? Fred, where's it gonna end?"

Fred rolled his eyes. "I didn't steal anything! Now knock it off. We gotta break outta here." He glanced around the cell, thinking hard.

Just then, there was a noise from outside.

A bark.

A *familiar* bark.

Fred lifted his head. "What the . . . ?" He

jumped to his feet and ran to the tiny window. "Dino?"

Sure enough, there was Dino, standing in the moonlight. He barked happily at Fred. Barney pushed up next to Fred so he could see.

"Dumb mutt," Fred grumbled, "following me all the way to Rock Vegas."

"Fred, that's not dumb!" Barney was excited. "I mean, if he's smart enough to find us here, maybe he's smart enough to help us get out!"

Fred brightened. "Barney, that's a great idea! Dino! Dino! Come here, boy. Come inside!" Fred kept calling until Dino ran around the building and found his way to the cell. When Dino saw Fred, he ran straight for him, squeezing through the bars, and jumped into his arms. He licked Fred's face over and over again. Dino was perfectly happy, now that he'd found Fred.

"Wait, wait," said Fred. "Shhh . . . Down, boy. Dino, see the keys? See the keys?" He pointed to a set of spare keys that were hanging on a row of hooks on the wall outside the cell. Dino turned to look, then looked back at Fred as if waiting for further instructions.

"Go get 'em. Go get the keys," Fred ordered.

Dino nodded. He trotted back out of the cell and over to the hooks on the wall. He looked up at them. They were too high to reach.

Fred shook his head sadly. It was no use. They'd rot in that cell.

But Dino trotted over to a chair by the desk. Using his nose, he pushed the chair over to the wall, beneath the row of keys. He climbed up on the chair, rose up shakily on his hind legs, and carefully picked up the set of keys.

Barney was overjoyed. "What'd I tell you, Fred? This is one smart puppy!"

"Yeah," Fred agreed. "I didn't know *what* he was up to with that chair." He called to Dino. "Okay, Dino. Now bring Daddy the keys."

Dino sat and wagged his tail. He was very proud of himself.

"No," said Fred. "No 'sit.' Come here."

Dino lifted a paw, as if to shake hands.

"Yes, good dog," Fred said, trying to be patient. "Very smart. Now bring the keys here."

Dino rolled over.

"No, Dino! Keys!"

Dino went into a dramatic death scene, then slumped to the ground, playing dead with all he had.

Barney was moved. He sniffled a little. "Hey, that was pretty good."

Just then, there was a sound outside. A loud meowing sound, the call of the saber-toothed tiger. Dino sat up straight with his ears perked. Then, without a backward glance, he dropped the keys and dashed out the door, taking off after the big cat. As the sounds of barking and meowing faded into the distance, Fred and Barney slumped back onto their bench.

CHAPTER EIGHTEEN
Pearl Rocks Vegas

I know, I know, you think it's about time for me, Gazoo, to make an entrance and save the day.

Soon, soon. First, let's head back to the hotel to see what's happening while Fred and Barney sit in prison.

Wilma was on the balcony of the suite, looking out over the lights of Rock Vegas. Suddenly, the door behind her banged open.

"Oh, my poor, poor baby!" Pearl Slaghoople cried and ran to hug Wilma. The Colonel wandered along behind her, looking a little dazed.

"Oh, perfect," said Wilma, rolling her eyes. Pearl was about the last person she needed to see at that moment.

"Everything's okay now," Pearl cooed, "Mother is here." She looked around the room. "What a dump," she added under her breath.

"Atten-*hup*!" cried the Colonel. In his mind, he was back in the army again.

"Hi, Daddy," said Wilma. It was actually comforting to see him.

"At ease, soldier," the Colonel answered, smiling fondly at his daughter.

"Mother, what are you doing here?" asked Wilma.

"Well, Chip let us know about your stolen necklace. My poor little girl! The victim of a crime!" Pearl looked upset.

"Oh, Mother." Wilma was exasperated. "You made this whole trip for nothing."

"Not necessarily," Pearl informed her. "There's a wonderful little fur boutique in the lobby."

Meanwhile, the Colonel was in the corner, talking to . . . a lamp. "You call that a clean uniform?" he bellowed. "Wipe that smile off your face, soldier!"

Ignoring him, Pearl pleaded with Wilma. "I can't stand by and watch you ruin your life. The first thing you're going to do is patch things up with Chip. Then I'll help you fix your hair for the Scones concert."

"It's the Stones, Mother. And you can have my ticket, because I'm leaving!" Wilma walked into the bedroom and began to throw clothes into her suitcase.

Pearl followed her. "Wilma, I've already talked to Chip, and he's willing to take you back."

Wilma was furious. "What gives you the right to interfere with my life?"

"I'm your mother. I love you. And Chip loves you."

Wilma made a face. "Chip loves *money*."

"And you have money!" Pearl said gaily. "It's a match made in heaven. Dear, don't you think he's proven his loyalty? He recovered a precious family heirloom for you, and at the same time rescued you from that beast."

"Fred is not a beast!" Wilma insisted. "He was just raised by them."

"Whatever." Pearl gave Wilma a serious look. "Wilma, it's time to grow up."

"Well, don't let me stop you," Wilma snapped. "Fred cares for me. I know he does."

"Chip cares enough to ask your father and me for your hand in marriage," Pearl pointed out. "The only thing Fred ever asked for was an extra dessert!"

"I will not allow you to speak about Fred Flintstone like that anymore." Wilma held up her head and left the bedroom.

"Wilma, nobody's perfect," Pearl admitted, following her. "Even I have made a mistake or two. I can admit that now. For example, I know I should have gone with stripes instead of spots in the guest room."

"Oh, how you've suffered," Wilma said sarcastically.

"I just don't want you to make a decision that'll haunt you for the rest of your life." Pearl paused. "Marry Chip, Wilma."

"No."

"Just think about it. If not for me, then for your poor, dear, frail father."

"That's not going to work this time, Mother," Wilma said, but her face softened when she looked at the Colonel, who was still talking to the lamp.

"Drop and give me fifty," he barked.

*　　*　　*

Meanwhile, upstairs in Chip's offices, Little Rocko and Big Rocko were getting serious. "I said, where's the money?" asked Big Rocko.

"You'll have it by midnight!" Chip promised.

"But I hear you aren't even dating that Slaghoople dame anymore," said Little Rocko.

"That's preposterous!" Chip looked desperate. "We're getting married this evening."

"Good," said Big Rocko. "But if for some reason the bride doesn't show, you're going to be in big trouble."

CHAPTER NINETEEN
Gazoo Saves the Day

Ta-daa! Ladies and gentlemen, the moment you've all been waiting for: I, Gazoo, am about to enter the scene!

Back at the prison, the neanderthal guard had come back — and promptly fell asleep. Now, he was snoring at the desk outside Fred and Barney's cell. Fred leaned against the bars, looking very depressed. Barney lay on his cot, playing one note over and over again on a harmonica.

"I miss Betty," he said.

"I know, Barn," Fred answered. "I'd do anything to see Wilma again. And we'd be with them right now, if I hadn't been so stupid." He banged his fist against the wall. "Stupid, stupid, stupid!"

"I could have told you that," I said, popping into view.

"Gazoo!" cried Barney.

"Gazoo!" echoed Fred. "Oh, boy, are you a sight for sore eyes. You gotta help us out, buddy! You gotta get us outta here!"

"Buddy?" I asked. "Did I hear that correctly? Buddy?" I looked at Fred. "I'm sorry, but aren't you the same Fred Flintstone who recently told me to fly my big nose back to the other side of the universe?" I sniffled a little, to show how much I was still hurting.

"You're right! You're right!" said Fred. "I was wrong. I tried to impress Wilma with money, and all I did was ruin everything. Like I always do." He shook his head. "I got nobody to blame but me. Because you know what I am? I'm nothing but a big —"

"Yes?" I asked.

"Dum-dum!" Fred finished.

"All opposed?" I asked, looking around. I didn't hear a peep. "The ayes have it."

Fred's head slumped down onto his chest.

"Wait, now," I said. "You've finally realized

what I knew all along. But that doesn't mean I haven't developed a little soft spot for you."

"Really?" asked Fred, sitting up straighter. "You mean you're gonna bust us outta here?"

"Ya-hoo!" yelled Barney. "Gazoo's gonna bust us out!"

"Whoa!" I cried, holding up my hands. "Do I look like the cavalry? You two must know that I can't actually interfere. I'd love to, but rules are rules. I'm only here to give you some information I thought you might find enlightening." I snapped my fingers, and a little movie screen (with its own projector, of course) appeared right next to me.

"Hey, I didn't know you could do that!" Fred looked amazed.

"You mean we coulda been watching wrestling this whole time?" Barney asked.

I tuned in the picture I wanted them to see. There was Chip, talking to the Rockos. *"See, by Sunday night,"* he was saying, *"I will be married to Wilma Slaghoople — heiress to one of the greatest personal fortunes in the uncivilized world . . ."*

Fred jumped up and rushed toward the

bars. He pulled at them, frantic. "Wilma's in trouble! We gotta get outta here!"

"Come on, Gazoo," Barney pleaded. "You gotta help us!"

"I wish I could. I really do." I meant it, too.

"So you're just gonna let this happen?" asked Fred. "We can't do anything about it? I'm supposed to sit here in this cell while Wilma walks down the aisle with the wrong guy? She's supposed to marry me! He doesn't even love her! We were supposed to live happily ever after . . ."

"Same with me and Betty," Barney chimed in. He started to cry. So did Fred. The two of them sat there, sobbing.

"Oh, no," I said desperately. "Please don't. Not — *emotions!* My race has prospered for eons without a trace of personal emotions, and we couldn't be happier." I paused for a second. "Well, we're not exactly happy, because happiness is an emotion, but . . ." I felt a sniffle coming on. And then I just couldn't help myself anymore. "But this is so sad! I need a hug!" I threw my arms around Fred's neck, and we cried together.

Barney, still crying, looked up to see a box of

tissues on the desk by the sleeping guard. Sniffling, he walked right through the bars and fetched the box. Then he walked back in and offered a tissue to Fred. "Here you go, buddy," he said.

Fred took a tissue and blew his nose. I never heard such a racket! "Thanks, pal," he said. He handed the box back to Barney.

Barney took a tissue and blew his nose, too. Then Fred realized what had just happened. "Barney!" he cried. Suddenly his tears had turned to laughter. "You can fit through the bars!"

"I can?"

"You just did it! To get the tissues. That means you can get us outta here!"

Barney chuckled. "How about that? I guess I should've tried that earlier, huh?"

"C'mon, c'mon!" Fred was impatient. "Get the keys!"

Barney walked through the bars again and tiptoed past the guard. He grabbed the keys and held them up for Fred to see. Then, as he was walking back to the cell, he stubbed his toe on one of the legs of the desk. "Ahhhh!" he cried.

The guard woke up. He looked straight at

Barney, who was hopping up and down, holding his foot.

"Hey!" said the guard. Even a neanderthal could see that something was wrong with this picture.

"Uh-oh," said Barney.

This was the moment of truth. Should I help them, even if it meant I'd be in trouble for "getting involved"? Hardly stopping to think, I faked a little sneeze. "Ah-chew!" I nodded my head toward a shelf over the desk, and it let loose. Everything on it, including a huge bowling trophy, came tumbling down. Right onto the guard's head. He fell over, unconscious.

Barney ran over to unlock the cell. "We did it!"

"Way to go, Barney!" said Fred. "Nice work, Gazoo!"

I looked toward the heavens, as if I could see my commander. "Don't listen to him!" I yelled. "I did nothing. *Nothing!*"

CHAPTER TWENTY
How High Can You Kick?

Back in Wilma and Betty's room, Betty was packing her suitcase. Wilma poked her head in the door. "I just came to say good-bye," she said. "I heard you're going to Stonehenge with Mick Jagged."

"Yeah," Betty said, in a flat tone. "I can't wait. I'm so excited." She started to cry. Then she looked up at Wilma. "Your mother's going around telling everyone that you're getting back together with Chip. I'm so happy for you."

That made Wilma start to cry. "No, Betty, I'm so happy for you," she insisted, sobbing as she spoke.

"I've never been so happy!" Betty was weeping.

"Oh, Betty," cried Wilma.

"Oh, Wilma!" cried Betty.

Tears rolling down their faces, they hugged.

"Hey!"

They turned to see Pearl Slaghoople standing in the doorway, with the Colonel behind her. "Don't be silly. You're big girls. Wilma, you're doing the right thing. I married the Colonel for his money, and look how happy I am."

The Colonel looked at a nearby lamp. "We meet again, soldier," he muttered.

"Chop-chop, Wilma," said Pearl. "You'll be late for the concert. Come, dear." She swept out of the room.

The Colonel came up to Wilma, who had collapsed onto the bed. "Chin up, soldier," he said. "Surrender is not an option."

"Thanks, Daddy." Wilma accepted his kiss. "I'm just so tired of fighting."

The Colonel whispered into her ear. "Then just do what I do," he said. "Pretend you're off your rocker, and everyone leaves you alone!"

Meanwhile, Fred and Barney approached the main door of the casino. Chip had already heard that they had escaped, and he'd provided all of his security guards with their pictures.

Fred noticed the guards checking everyone over. "They're looking for us, Barn," he said. "They've got guards everywhere."

"So what are we gonna do?" asked Barney.

Fred thought for a moment. "I have to see Wilma, and you gotta find Betty. We're just gonna have to fight our way in." He couldn't come up with a plan that sounded better.

Barney wasn't crazy about that idea. The guards looked pretty tough. "Can we try one of my ideas first for a change?" asked Barney. He'd just spotted two guys pushing a rack of showgirl costumes past them.

A few minutes later, backstage in the casino's main lounge, a man knocked on a dressing-room door. "Come on, girls! Let's move! The curtain's going up!"

The door flew open, and a group of showgirls piled out of the room, all dressed in shiny, sequined outfits and towering feathered head-dresses. As they passed the guards who were patrolling backstage, they separated into two lines.

There, right in the middle of one of the lines, were Fred and Barney.

In sequins and feathers.

"I think we made it in," said Barney, looking back at the guards.

"Me, too," said Fred. He started to take off his headdress.

They were just about to take off in the other direction, when suddenly the curtain went up.

"Ladies and gentlemen," an announcer cried. "The Tardust is proud to present the world famous Rockettes!"

Music started to play and the line of show-girls linked arms and danced out onto the stage, kicking all the way. Fred and Barney couldn't escape. They were pulled right along with the others.

The crowd applauded as the kicking dancers appeared. Fred and Barney tried to blend in, but it wasn't easy. Especially since Fred's headdress kept falling off.

Still, so far so good.

Then, disaster struck. It was time for each dancer to do a solo. They stepped out one at a time to show off their stuff, and each one had fancier moves than the one before. They did super high kicks, somersaults, flips, backflips . . . the crowd was going nuts.

Suddenly, it was Barney's turn. He stepped out sheepishly and hopped up and down on one foot. The audience clapped weakly. Then Fred came forward, doing his "twinkle-toe" walk, the one he used for bowling. He tried a wobbly spin — and fell over, back into the line.

That did it.

The entire line of dancers went down like dominos, leaving Fred and Barney standing there on their own.

"Hey, it's the escapees!" shouted a guard. "Stop them!" A bunch of guards ran after Barney and Fred, who dashed backstage and up the stairs.

Fred and Barney ran, still dressed in their outfits, across a high catwalk — only to discover another group of guards coming up toward them from the other side.

They were trapped.

Fred looked at Barney. Barney looked at Fred.

"Gee, Fred," said Barney. "I hope we're back in jail in time for dinner."

"We're not finished yet." Fred turned. "Follow me!" He leaped off the catwalk, grabbed onto a vine that was attached to a pulley, and lowered himself to the floor.

The guards came closer to Barney. He leapt, too, but the vine he grabbed was the other end of Fred's. "Whoa!" he cried as he was yanked up and over the railing the vine was hung on. "Whoa!" he cried again as he plummeted toward the floor and landed with a crash next to Fred.

He picked himself up and dusted himself off. "Let's go find Mick Jagged's dressing room before those guys catch up with us again," he said. He took off, with Fred behind him.

They burst into the dressing room to find Mick showing off his dance moves to Betty.

"Barney? Fred?" asked Betty.

"Wow," said Fred. "You really *do* know Mick Jagged."

"Who are you?" asked Mick, glaring at Fred and Barney.

"The cuter one used to be my boyfriend," Betty told him.

Barney's face fell. "It's okay, Betty. I understand if you wanna be with some famous rock star instead of me. I just wanted to come back to tell you that I love you. I don't think I ever actually told you that. But now I did, so . . . 'bye." He turned to leave.

"Barney, wait!" Betty cried. "Do you mean it?"

Barney turned back. "Of course I do. I've never felt this way about anybody before. You know that."

Betty was still upset. "What about that girl you were with at the all-you-can-eat buffet?"

"Roxie? She's Chip Rockefeller's girlfriend," Barney answered.

"Chip Rockefeller has a girlfriend?" asked Betty. "Somebody better tell Wilma!"

"Don't worry, Betty," said Fred. "I'll handle Rockefeller." He peeked out of the dressing room door, into the main lounge. There was Wilma, sitting at Rockefeller's table with him. Fred saw Chip put his hand over Wilma's. She frowned, but she didn't move her hand away. Fred watched, deep in thought. How was he going to prove his love to Wilma?

From behind him, Mick spoke up. "Would somebody mind telling me what is going on here?"

"I'm sorry, Mick," said Betty. "I've had a really good time with you, but . . . I love Barney."

"Ya-hoo!" Barney opened his arms wide, and Betty ran into them.

"Oh, yeah?" asked Mick. "Well, I don't care. I love you, Betty! You're the first decent, honorable woman I've ever met, and I must have you!"

"You better watch out, pal," said Barney, "or I'm gonna give you a fat lip. On second thought, it looks like somebody already did!"

Betty cracked up. She and Barney laughed together, looking into each other's eyes. It was like when they first met. Magic.

Mick was furious. "That's it!" he cried. "Nobody steals a bird from me after I've gone to all the trouble of stealing her from him!" He dove toward Barney, and they wrestled for a moment.

"Barney!" cried Betty.

"Betty's mine, Mick!" shouted Barney.

"Oh, yeah? Over my dead body!" yelled Mick.

Barney picked up a guitar and broke it over Mick's head, knocking him out cold.

"Go, Barn!" said Fred. He peeked out at the audience again, then back into the dressing room. His eye fell on Mick's wild stage costume. It was

127

fuchsia, full length, with feathers all over it. Fred stared at it. Should he? Could he?

Betty and Barney were hugging. "Oh, Barney, I've missed you so much!" Betty said, sighing happily.

"Me too." Barney grinned. "I mean, I've missed *you*, Betty."

There was a knock on the door. "Mick, you're onstage in five minutes," called a stagehand.

Betty and Barney looked down at Mick, who was still out cold. "Uh-oh," said Betty. "What do we do now?"

"And where did Fred go?" asked Barney. He looked up and noticed the hanger Mick's costume had been on. Now it was empty. "I've got a bad feeling about this," he said.

CHAPTER TWENTY-ONE
Happily Ever After

Out in the lounge, the audience was getting restless.

"Bring on the Stones! Bring on the Stones!" they chanted.

Chip Rockefeller checked his watch. Then he slid closer to Wilma. "Wilma," he said, "I love you. I always have. I lost you once, but I won't lose you again. Marry me, tonight!"

"Oh, Chip," said Wilma. "So much has happened. I need time to think."

Chip looked across the room to see Big Rocko glaring at him. He swallowed nervously. "Wilma, please! I can't *live* without you. Just say yes! Please!"

Fortunately for Wilma, the lights went dim

just then and a voice boomed out, "Ladies and gentlemen! The Tardust is proud to present the world's greatest — and only — rock band . . . Mick Jagged and the Stonnnnnes!"

The crowd went wild. On the stage, a giant clamshell opened up to reveal the Stones. Lights flashed all over, and then a spotlight came to rest at the empty spot near a microphone.

A figure rose from beneath the stage. Mick!

But was it? He looked a little . . . heavy. His back was to the audience as the music began. He twitched his hips. Then he whipped around to face the crowd.

It was . . . Fred.

Wilma looked stunned. Fred gazed out at her, and their eyes met. He leaned into the microphone and began to sing.

He sang a love song, a song that they'd heard on the night they met. He crooned it to Wilma, staring into her eyes the whole time. Then the guitar solo began, and he worked his way over to Chip's table. As the guitar played, he spoke into the microphone.

"Wilma, honey," he said, "I never meant to

hurt you. I've done some stupid things — heck, I've done a *lot* of stupid things. But love makes you do stupid things." By then, he was at the table, standing right next to her.

"And Wilma," he went on, "I know you're free to choose how you wanna live your life, and who you wanna live it with. You may never forgive me, but I'd never forgive myself if I didn't give this one last try."

Fred got down on one knee.

"Wilma Slaghoople, I can't give you diamonds, or fast cars, or fancy houses . . . All I can give you is just plain old Fred Flintstone from Bedrock, and all the love in my heart. I hope that's enough."

He looked up at her. "Wilma, will you . . . will you . . ."

Would you believe it? Fred picked that moment to lose his nerve. He began to sweat and stammer and — I couldn't take it anymore. I popped up behind him and give him a good swift kick.

That did the trick.

"Wilma, will you marry me?" asked Fred.

The band stopped playing and the crowd fell silent. Wilma looked at Fred with tears in her eyes.

Chip tapped Wilma on the shoulder. "Uh, Wilma?" he asked. "I'm still waiting . . ."

Wilma looked at him blankly. Then she looked back at Fred. "Yes," she said.

"To me or to him?" asked Chip.

"To him!" cried Wilma.

Fred jumped up. "YABBA DABBA DOO!" he cried.

The crowd burst into cheers and applause. Fred and Wilma hugged, and as the band began to play again, everybody in the place sang along.

Fred and Wilma were married the very next day, beneath a beautiful, flower-bedecked gazebo near the Tardust pool. Wilma looked stunning in her long white gown, and Fred was dashing in tails. Betty was the maid of honor and Barney, of course, was the best man. Everybody was there: Pearl and the Colonel, Roxie, Dino . . . and me, Gazoo.

"Do you," asked the justice of the peace, "Fred Flintstone, take Wilma Slaghoople to be your wife? To have and to hold from this day forward?"

"I yabba-dabba-do!" said Fred, beaming at Wilma, who had already promised to be his wife.

"Then, by the power vested in me by the City of Rock Vegas, I now pronounce you husband and wife. You may kiss the bride."

Their kiss was about the most romantic thing I've ever seen. Pearl must have been overwhelmed, too: She fell right into the pool.

I'm not too proud to admit that I shed a tear or two.

"Gazoo?" asked Barney. "Are you crying?"

"Of course not, dum-dum," I said. "I'm simply overcome with . . . information. It's just that I finally understand your complex marriage rituals. All the emotions. All the . . . love. And I've come to the conclusion that . . ." I couldn't help myself anymore. I began to weep. "I'll never meet anybody!"

Dino surprised me with a huge lick on my cheek.

"You're very sweet," I told him, sniffling, "but believe me, it would never work out."

The justice of the peace turned to the crowd. "Ladies and gentlemen," he said, "I now present to you Mr. and Mrs. Flintstone!" Wilma tossed her bouquet, and, naturally, Betty caught it. Barney gave Betty a big kiss.

Then, as the Stones began to play and fireworks thundered over Rock Vegas, Fred and Wilma Flintstone walked down the aisle, both of them smiling from ear to ear.

CHAPTER TWENTY-TWO
And a Happy Gazoo, Too

The next day, I stood out in the middle of the desert, waiting for the mother ship to pick me up.

The skies were empty.

"Okay," I called. "I'm ready! I know I may have overstepped my bounds just a wee bit, but I think you'll be very pleased with my report."

I waited.

Nothing.

"Uh, I'm ready to go home now! Really ready . . ."

There was no response.

"I'm waiting! Any day now . . . Beam me up! Hellooooo! Okay, joke's over . . . uh, aren't you forgetting somebody! I'm right here! Gazoo phone home?"

I danced around a little, hoping to be spotted.

There still wasn't a peep from above.

Then I turned to see the most attractive being I'd yet noticed on earth. It was tall, and green, and prickly all over. I think I've heard it referred to as a "cactus." I walked over to it.

"Well, *hello*," I said. It just goes to show you. Maybe I was wrong about never meeting anybody, after all.